THE HAWAIIAN ISLAND DETECTIVE CLUB SERIES

Pineapples in Peril

BY Cheryl Linn Martin

Comfort PUBLISHING

For information, address Comfort Publishing, 296 Church St. N., Concord, NC 28025. The views expressed in this book are not necessarily those of the publisher.

This book is a work of fiction. All characters contained herein are fictitious, or if real, are used fictitiously and have no bearing on their actual behavior.

First printing

Book cover design
by Reed Karriker

ISBN: 978-1-936695-48-5
Published by Comfort Publishing, LLC
www.comfortpublishing.com

Printed in the United States of America

To my parents, Betty and Gordon,
who would have loved seeing my stories in print.

Acknowledgements

Above all, I give my gratitude and praise to God who has been with me every step, no matter how difficult, along this amazing writing journey.

My family has been an incredible support team, each in their own way. Thank you to my husband, Harrison, my children, Ian, Ashley, and Shane, and my son-in-law, Dave.

A huge thank-you to my agent, Terry Burns of Hartline Literary, for his unending support and perseverance to see *The Hawaiian Island Detective Club* series published. And I would not be in this position today without Terry's editorial assistant (now an agent with Hartline), Linda Glaz, who fell in love with *Pineapples in Peril,* and brought it to Terry.

Critique groups are vital to the success of any writer. Becoming an author is a long process filled with ups and downs. A great critique group helps you navigate the maze of frustrations and sees you through to the finish line. Thank you, Karla Akins, Camille Eide, Linda Glaz, Emily Hendrickson, Jessica Nelson, and former partners, Kellie Gilbert and RanDee Hill.

And what would I do without a reader from my target age group to offer their opinion? I asked two boys, one in the eight-year-old range and one in the twelve-year-old range to read *Pineapples in Peril*. Thanks, Zachary and Dak, for reading and loving my story.

Thank you, members of American Christian Fiction Writers, Oregon Christian Writers, and the Portland Chapter of ACFW, for all your support, instruction and opportunities.

Finally, thank you, Kristy Huddle, and everyone at Comfort Publishing who were willing to take the risk with a new author, and publish *The Hawaiian Island Detective Club* series.

Pronunciation Help for Some of the Hawaiian Words Used in *Pineapples in Peril*

Leilani is pronounced: lay-LAH-nee
Kimo is pronounced: KEE-moh
Akamai is pronounced: ah-kah-MY
Maile is pronounced: MY-lee
Kainoa is pronounced: ky-NO-ah (ky rhymes with sky.)
Luana is pronounced: lu-AHN-ah
Onakea is pronounced: oh-nah-KAY-ah

Other Words
(and Some Meanings)

Hukilau is pronounced: HOO-kee-lau (lau rhymes with cow.)
Meaning: Huki—pull Lau—leaves (ti leaves) used to line the fishing net. The hukilau song and hula is about fishing and a fishing party.

Imu is pronounced: EE-moo
Meaning: The underground pit that is an oven with hot rocks for cooking a whole pig.

Kilauea is pronounced: keel-ah-WAY-ah
Meaning: The active volcano (southeastern slope of Mauna Loa) on the big island of Hawaii.
Lanai is pronounced: la-NY (NY rhymes with sky.)
Meaning: A porch or veranda.

Lei is pronounced: LAY
Meaning: A garland of flowers or leaves to be worn.

Luau is pronounced: LOO-au (au rhymes with cow.)
Meaning: A Hawaiian feast.

Mahalo is pronounced: ma-HA-loh
Meaning: Thank you.

Tutu is pronounced: TOO-too (There is no "T" in the Hawaiian alphabet, but the "T" is a hold-over from Tahitian and other Polynesian languages.)
Meaning: An endearing term for Grandma.

Some of the Foods Mentioned

Char Siu Bao is a Chinese bun with a pork center, pronounced: CHAR SOO BOH (BOH rhymes with go.)
Kalua (Pig) is the Hawaiian imu-cooked pork, pronounced: kah-LOO-ah
Lomi (Salmon) is the Hawaiian tomato and salmon salad, pronounced: LOH-mee

Ekahi
(One)

I leapt off the lanai, dodged between two palms and pow-
ered through the rows of pineapples. The perfect getaway, but a
quick peek over my shoulder proved I was not in the safety zone
yet. My brother, Kimo, bounded out of the house and across the
sand, sprays of the grit billowing up behind him.

Oh man, he'd seen me! I'd been so careful, but the little
twit must have been hiding somewhere, watching. I used the
anger to propel me faster. The Hawaiian sun blazed down on my
bare arms and legs. Trying to ignore the heat, I blasted through
the spiky leaves, eyes set on the road just beyond the pineapple
fields.

Strands of hair escaped my flopping, dark brown ponytail
and stuck to my glossed lips. The small backpack, strung loosely
on my shoulders, slapped with each pounding step. Sucking in
a major breath of fruity air, I stretched each stride further and
increased my lead. But how long would I have to run before my
little brother would give up the chase? He seemed to have made
it his life's mission to irritate and frustrate me. Why couldn't he
just leave me alone? This was my stuff — my life — not his.

Determined to leave him far behind, I pushed harder, ignoring
the pain in my chest and the burning in my throat.

"You're in big trouble, Leilani!" Kimo's ten-year-old, high-pitched squeal barely reached my ears. He always told Mom I was mean to him. Why did he want to tag along with me and my friends anyway?

I wanted to yell back, to tell him Mom would side with me, but was too busy trying to breathe. I hoped I could continue at this pace and not pass out. Glancing over my shoulder, I saw Kimo retreating. I smiled and faced forward, pleased I had won the battle.

Suddenly, I spotted a rock resting in the middle of my path. *Jump, Leilani!*

Too late. My flip-flop caught on the stone, bulleting me forward. I face-planted between rows of prickly fruit and into dirt mixed with remains of molding, smashed pineapples. I groaned and rolled to the side. "Ouuuuch!" Everything hurt, especially my face and arms.

I opened one eye and wiped a hand across my face. Bits of sandy soil and squished pineapple fell to the ground. The taste of fruit and dirt hung on my lips. Spitting, I tried to rid my mouth of the foul gunk. Great. I probably looked like a zombie, fresh from the grave. I moved, but pain shot through my left arm. "Owie, owie, owie!" Grabbing my wrist, I prayed the horrible aching would stop. Oh, no! Maybe I broke the stupid thing. Perfect way to start eighth grade. Leilani Akamai in a cast — no surfing, no snorkeling, no wakeboarding.

I winced and held my left wrist against my body. Hoisting myself into a sitting position with my good arm, I noticed my slippers. One rested upside down under a pineapple plant, the other hung on the edge of the evil rock. I scooted on my behind and reached for them. The flip-flops were still out of range, so I inched a little more until I could grab them and slip my toes in.

This was all Kimo's fault. I pushed against the ground with my good arm and leveraged myself into a standing position. *Sorry, God, but my little brother is super annoying.* Mom always reminded me Kimo was a special blessing. Ha! I'd never seen any proof.

Okay, so I was standing — covered with grit and streaks of blood, and protecting an injured arm. At least both legs seemed to work. I thought about calling Maile or my mom, but remembered my cell was at home, charging.

I hobbled the rest of the way through the fields. It seemed the pineapples stretched ahead forever. After endless steps, I finally reached the road, turned and inched toward Maile's special place. I had no idea how long I'd been shuffling along. My best friend was going to be ticked. Had she waited for me or given up and gone home?

As soon as the cluster of palms near the beach came into view, I hollered. No use trudging any further if she'd already given up. "Hey, Maile! You there?"

My friend edged out from the shadows. Her long, dark hair flittered in the tropical breeze. Even from a distance I saw the sun sparkling off the auburn strands that danced among the dark ones.

"Leilani?" She trotted toward me. "You okay?"

"Yeah." I moved my left arm and cringed. "Uh, maybe not."

"Oh man! What happened to you? You're a mess."

"Thanks."

Maile chuckled. "Sorry. But I was beginning to think you were a real flake, calling me to meet you and then bailing."

I gulped a deep breath and repositioned my arm. "Figured you would."

"I called your cell, but you didn't answer."

"Yeah. It's at the house."

Maile grabbed my right elbow. "Let's go. You need to get home and to the doctor."

I shook my head. "No, not yet. You have to see what I found." I nodded toward our spot in the palms. "Let's get out of the sun and sit down."

"You got it." She dragged me along. "You sure you don't want to head to my house? My mom can drive you home."

I shook my head. "I'll live."

"You never told me what happened. Run into an erupting volcano or something?"

Even grinning at my best friend hurt. Maile Onakea always had something to say to make me laugh. "Just being a klutz."

We made it to the shade. "You lie. You couldn't be a klutz if you tried."

Maile was right. All the surfing and my sturdy Hawaiian build had made me pretty tough and coordinated. "Yeah, well, actually, it was Kimo."

"Kimo? How could this possibly be your dorky little brother's fault?"

I wiggled my shoulders, trying to get the backpack straps to fall to the sides. "Can you help me get this off?"

"Sure." She reached for the pack and slid it down.

I cringed as I adjusted my arm. Pain shot from my wrist to my shoulder. "He was chasing me. Then I tripped on some stupid rock."

"Ouch!" Maile winced. "Okay, Leilani, what's so important that you would hurt yourself trying to get here?"

I wondered the same thing. Maybe I was totally lame. Would she see the importance in the news story?

I tried to unzip my bag — hard to do with one hand. I sighed and gave up the mission.

"Let me get it." Maile grabbed the backpack, opened it and pulled out several things. "I see you're traveling with all the essentials." She waved each item and snickered. "Brush…lip gloss…mirror…mascara."

Snatching the thin black tube, I sneered at my friend. "Okay, very funny." It wasn't fair. Maile could go totally natural and look so cute. Not me. I needed a lot of help, and then I might be okay, but never cute.

"Sorry!" My friend raised her hands in mock surrender. She peered into the bag. "So, what exactly am I looking for?"

"A newspaper article."

She rummaged through my *essentials*. "I don't…Wait, I think I've got it." She pulled out the crumpled newsprint and waved it in front of me.

"Yup. You found it. Now read it."

"Sure." Maile smoothed the rumples and cleared her throat. Stretching up as tall as she could — which wasn't much — she cocked her head and read.

Pineapple Vandals Strike Again

On Friday night, June 25, the Tong Pineapple Plantation suffered damage at the hands of unidentified vandals for the second time this summer. Hundreds of immature fruit were found cut from plants, ripe ones smashed between rows.

Officer Matthew Emerson of the local police force stated, "The damage could be the result of teenagers seeking thrills. They may not understand the financial implications of their destructive behavior."

Plantation owner, William Tong, is offering a reward for details leading to the identity of the culprits. Contact the police if you have any information regarding this crime.

Maile stared at me. "This is what you almost killed yourself over?"

"Don't you get it?" Trying to ignore the throbbing in my arm, I shifted my position. "This is what we've been waiting for — a chance to do a real investigation."

Maile grimaced. "Yeah, for you, maybe. You're the mystery nut, not me. Besides, we've outgrown the Detective Club thing."

"Yeah, for sure. But this isn't like when we read all those books and pretended. This is a real crime."

She giggled. "You dork."

I flashed a fiery stare at my friend. Didn't she get it? This was our chance to prove we were real detectives with skills to investigate, evaluate and solve. "The police don't care about this vandalism. They think it's just teenagers and it'll all go away once the thrill is gone." Sighing, I loaded my stuff into my bag. "Fine. You don't want to help, but I'm solving this case."

I stole a sideways glance at Maile. Maybe I could convince her if I mentioned the money thing. I totally wanted to take horseback riding lessons, and get a second surfboard — a soft top —so I didn't always have to use my seven-foot longboard when I was tackling more difficult waves. I crashed and burned a lot. "And just think of all the reward money. You could get the new wakeboard you've been wanting."

She stared at me, then grinned. "I was also kinda liking a swimsuit and matching sundress I saw the other day..." She sighed. "Okay, I'm in, but only if we get Sam to help us."

Beaming, I bounced up and down, but then winced in pain. *Oh, man, this stupid arm!* "Of course we'll get Sam in on it. I tried to call him, but he was at the beach."

Maile zipped my backpack. "I'll carry this for you. We need to get you to my house."

"I can make it home. I'm good."

"Yeah, but your house is too far away." She helped me up.

Everything had gone stiff. Groaning, I held my injured arm across my stomach.

Maile laughed, and I couldn't help but join her as I pictured what I must look like. She grabbed my right wrist and we rounded the palm.

I froze.

We stood face to face with our dreaded enemy, Carly Rivers. My stomach churned, but not because of physical pain. She was hanging on the arm of Maile's older brother, Kainoa. Dark skin, streaky sun-bleached hair and amazing muscles, he was the hunkiest surfer on the Hawaiian Islands.

And the love of my life.

Elua
(Two)

"Hi, there!" Carly's smile was Miss America perfect. Her cropped blonde hair stood out against tanned skin — also perfect. "What are you two cuties up to?"

Cuties? Just because she was 16, she had no right to call us that — like we were little kids or something. Maile turned 13 last March, and my birthday had been three weeks ago. We were teenagers, just like her. My stomach cramped, and even with support, my arm throbbed.

"Oh my! What happened to you?" She reached toward my left side. "You okay?"

I ignored the pain and put on the best I'm-super-tough expression I could manage. "I'm fine. We're heading back to Maile's."

"Hey, sistah. Mo' bettah you stay home."

I loved it when Kainoa spoke Pidgin English. He mostly used it when hanging with his surfer friends, but I wished he'd speak it more. He was so cute. Did Miss I'm-totally-sophisticated Carly appreciate it?

Maile planted both hands on her hips. "We're heading home right now. Mom mad or something?"

Kainoa shrugged. "Kinda. She needs help with the chicken long rice."

"Oh yeah, the church potluck." Maile pulled me along. "On our way." Then she stopped. "Maybe I should call her."

I glanced back and frowned at the sight of Carly and Kainoa strolling through the grass and palms toward the beach. What did he see in her anyway? Maybe she was model perfect, but could she snorkel, surf or boogieboard? Maybe she could waltz along the shore, but could she plow through the sand and leap to catch a mid-flight Frisbee?

Maile reached in her pocket and tugged on her cell. "Can you believe my brother is with Carly?"

I sighed. "Yeah. What a bummer."

She yanked harder on the phone. Her tight capris held it captive. The phone popped out from the khaki vice-grip and flew through the air, smacking into a palm tree and exploding into a mega number of pieces. "Oh, man!" She marched to the tree and scooped up the mess. "I think it's a goner."

I frowned. "Sorry about your phone, but it's okay. I can walk to your house."

Maile trudged back and linked arms with me. "Mom's going to kill me. This is the second phone I've destroyed in two months."

"Serial phone killer, huh?"

"Doubt Mom will find it funny." She puffed out a blast of air as we plodded down the road. "Anyway, about my brother. I figure Carly's just charming him to death."

"He's never fallen for sappy stuff before." The Kainoa I knew loved surfing — wind, body and board — and barely smiled at girls.

"My brother's been a little girl-crazy lately." Maile shrugged. " 'Course, it would be nice if she wasn't our uppity neighbor."

"I don't get it. Doesn't he remember all the stuff she did to us, and how mean and rude she was?" Still snotty, she'd talked down to us like we were nothing compared to her.

"Doubt it." Maile quick-stepped ahead of me, turned and wagged her finger. "Why is Kainoa's infatuation so important?" She walked backward and cocked her head. "You jealous?"

Heat rushed to my face and burned in my cheeks. "No." I shrugged. "I mean, he's kinda cool and all, but…"

Maile whipped around to face forward again, and linked her elbow with mine. "Yes you are." She giggled. "My brother is such a –" She swayed as if catching a wave, and put on her best guy voice. "I'm-the-greatest-surfer-dude-ever."

I chuckled, then groaned. "Owie! Don't make me laugh. It hurts when my arm moves."

"Sorry." She cupped her hand over her mouth.

We walked a while in silence until Maile smacked her hand against her forehead. "I think I get it. You like the surfer-dude type. You have lots in common with Kainoa."

I shrugged. Maile could never really understand. He was her brother. She thought of him as a nerd, only interested in surfing, his tan and working out. She didn't see the sweet, friendly person I saw. He'd always encouraged me in my surfing, and gave me hints on tackling better and longer rides on larger waves.

"It's okay, Leilani. There are lots of cool guys our age." She nudged up against me. "Including surfers."

I smiled. Nope, she didn't get it. No one could ever match Kainoa.

We approached the Onakea home. Open and airy, it sat back from the road. Palms, mango and plumeria filled the land and draped the path. I drew a long breath of the sweet scent.

"Mahhhhm!" After yelling, Maile stopped, waited a moment, then turned and leveled her eyes with mine. "Wait here. I'll run and get her."

She jogged about halfway when Mrs. O appeared on the lanai, wiping her hands on a kitchen towel. She was older and heavier than my mom, but still pretty. Her brown eyes spit fire when she was mad, just like Maile's.

"Where have you been? I told you I needed your help today."

"Sorry. But Leilani is hurt. Can we take her home so she can get to the doctor?"

Her mom hustled down the stairs. "Good heavens. Why didn't you call me?" She paused. "You do have your phone, right?"

"Yeah…" My friend reached in her pocket and pulled out several pieces.

"Oh, Maile, not another one!" She sighed, turned and plodded toward the house.

I leaned in close and whispered in her ear. "So far, so good. Your mom hasn't killed you yet." I tried to stifle a giggle, but it escaped as a snort.

"Just wait." Maile sighed. "Promise me you'll drop the pineapple case and investigate my murder, okay?"

I laughed, then grabbed my arm and moaned in pain.

We reached the screened lanai, opened the door and sauntered into the house. Mrs. O was on the phone talking with my mom. From the one side of the conversation that I could hear, I knew I was in as much trouble as my friend. I nudged her. "It's going to be hard for me to investigate anything if I'm dead too."

A huge grin overtook her face. "Go sit on the couch and I'll bring you some ice."

Mrs. O hung up the phone and waved her hand. "Already made an ice pack." She picked up the plastic bag, wrapped it in a towel and placed it on my arm. "You okay, dear?"

Cold comfort penetrated. It seemed to soothe my aching heart as well as the stabbing pain. "Yeah. I'm good. Thanks." I worked my way to the couch and settled into soft cushions.

"Your mom should be here in about ten minutes." Hands on hips, Mrs. O stood in front of me. She looked me over, then bent to zoom in closer. "Looks like you've swallowed a bit of dirt. Bet your mouth's dry, huh? I'll get some orange-papaya juice." She headed for the kitchen.

Maile settled onto the sofa, next to me. "So, what do you think our first move in this pineapple thing should be?"

"Don't know." Whatever I planned next had better be good, something to make up for the horrible day so far. "Can you call Sam and see if he can meet us at my house tonight?"

She shook her head. "Won't work. Church potluck."

I heaved out a lungful of air. "Right." Mom was really going to be irritated about my accident since she was probably in the middle of making a guava cake.

Maile's mom approached with a large glass of juice. "This ought to help."

"Thanks, Mrs. O." I grabbed the glass and downed several gulps, thankful I hadn't injured my right arm. If I had, I'd have been stuck using my uncoordinated left hand to drink. I frowned at the vision of juice dribbling from my mouth and hang-gliding onto my tank-top. 'Course, with my luck, Kainoa would have walked in just in time to see the whole slobbery waterfall thing.

"Maile, keep Leilani company, but after her mom arrives, I expect you to help me cook."

"Sure, Mom."

I shifted my position, careful to keep the ice and arm still. "I just thought of something. Why don't we meet Sam at the potluck? We could hang out in the preschool room and make a plan."

"Great idea. I'll call him later."

"I'll think about the case and come up with some ideas."

"Okay, but don't forget to write everything down. Do you have an extra spiral at home?"

"Yup." The ice must have been working well because the throbbing seemed to have disappeared. Now my mind could concentrate on the investigation rather than the pain. Where should we start? Suspects. We'd make a list. Motives. Much easier. Most crimes seemed to involve greed, passion, power or thrill. I couldn't wait to write my ideas in a notebook.

My thoughts were interrupted by a rumbling outside. "I hear a motor." I scooted to the edge of the couch, stood and trudged through the kitchen toward the lanai. Mom's car approached. "Thanks, Mrs. O, for all your help." Placing the ice pack on the counter, I watched my mom climb out of the black SUV. She was taller than me, but thinner. I took after my dad with broad Hawaiian shoulders and chest, my arms and legs strong and toned from all the surfing.

Mom wore her blonde hair pulled back, swirled and clipped into a loose clump. Little spikes of hair stuck out on top like a peacock tail.

She trotted up the stairs and spotted me as she opened the door. "Leilani, what on earth happened to you? You okay, sweetie?"

I moved onto the lanai and nodded. "I tripped. And my arm really hurts."

She placed a gentle hand under my chin. "I can't imagine you being so clumsy."

"It's all Kimo's fault, Mom. I was running because he was follow –"

Her palm flashed in front of my face. "Stop it right there, missy. Kimo is not to blame for every misadventure in your life. And why didn't you call me?"

I cringed. The lecture was coming. "I left my cell at home."

"You, missy, need to remember your phone." Mom planted both hands on her hips. "Would you like me to confiscate it? Apparently you don't really want it since you never take it with you." She sighed. "You're going to get into real trouble one of these days. Then what would you do without a phone to call for help?"

"Sorry."

Her arms fell to her sides and she spoke softly. "Now, get your stuff and let's go."

Frowning, I turned. Maile stood in the kitchen, holding my backpack. I snatched it and passed her a slight smile. "Thanks. See you tonight." I'd always loved mysteries. It was fun pretending, but this was a chance to prove I could be a true detective and solve a real crime.

"You bet."

Mom touched Mrs. O's arm. "Thank you, Luana."

She nodded. "No problem. I figure we kind of share these two girls." She chuckled. "Otherwise, how would we ever get them to adulthood?"

My mom smiled. "You have a point."

"Olivia, are you making your famous guava cake for the church dinner?"

"Yes." Mom shot me a big dose of evil-eye. "I was in the middle of mixing batter when you called." She returned her gaze to Mrs. O. "We might not make it tonight with what's happened to Leilani, so please give my regrets to everyone."

I swallowed hard and shuddered. Not make it? How could she say that? We had to go. Meeting tonight with Maile and

Sam was mega-important. The trail to catching the culprits would turn cold soon. Pressing my lips tight, I shot Maile what I hoped to be the most firm, strong-minded expression I could muster. "Don't worry. I'll be there."

Determined to make it to the church for our meeting, I turned and tramped after my mom.

Climbing into the huge truck and buckling up involved more effort than I expected. Mom helped, but remained silent. She seemed totally mad. I stayed silent too.

Once we were off the property and on our way down the main road, I decided to try my luck with her. "I'm sure we can still go to the dinner tonight."

"I wouldn't count on it. You may have to get a cast. Are you still in a lot of pain?"

I shook my head. "Not too much."

"I wouldn't be surprised if you broke it." She glanced in the rearview mirror. "Why are you so worried about the pot-luck, anyway? It's not like you've ever been much interested in church functions."

How could I answer without sounding totally lame or letting her know our plan? "Maile and Sam will be there, and we planned on hanging out."

"Well, you may just have to *hang out* some other time." She pushed the gas pedal and we zoomed down the open road. "We need to stop at the house before going to the clinic."

"Why?"

"I was so upset after Luana called, I made a rash decision to leave Kimo at home alone."

"I'm sure he's fine."

"Yeah. He was pretty excited to be on his own." She turned into our driveway. "Exactly what worries me."

Mom unbuckled and jumped onto the ground. I struggled with the seatbelt, frustrated that she'd said we might not make it to the potluck. Maile, Sam and I had to plan our investigation right away so we could find fresh clues and evidence. Finally I released the seatbelt's grip as my mom opened the front door.

"Oh, no! Kimo!"

Lightning bolts shot through me at the sound of Mom's yelling. What happened? I slid out of the truck and ran toward the house, ignoring the pain shooting through my arm. Peering around my mom, I caught sight of Kimo…and the evidence of an explosion all over him.

Ekolu
(Three)

Pink liquid matted with flour slithered down Kimo's face and shirt.

Mom raised her hands and scanned the room. "What happened?"

I followed her past my brother and into the kitchen. Spatters of pink and white decorated walls, fridge and stove.

"I was trying to help you finish the cake." Kimo wiped away thick goop from his forehead. "I put the powder in the mixing machine with the watery stuff you already made, but when I turned it on…"

"Oh, Kimo, you didn't!" Mom stared at her beloved red Kitchen Aid, now drenched in slime.

"I wanted to make you happy and finish the cake for tonight."

Mom passed him a wary smile and grabbed a kitchen towel. "I know." She wiped his face and shoulders. "You can't put all the liquid and flour in the mixer at once, honey. I'm making two cakes, so you have to split everything. Otherwise it's too much for the mixer to handle."

"Oh." Kimo spoke to the floor.

I felt kind of sorry for him. He really tried to help. But I worried about letting my guard down too much. He was still my annoying little brother.

Mom panned the kitchen once again and sighed. "What speed did you use?"

"I turned it up all the way. I wanted to make sure it mixed up real good. But it started whipping everything out of the bowl and all around."

I grimaced and shook my head. "So why didn't you turn the thing off?"

Kimo whimpered. "I tried, but the cake stuff was in my eyes and I couldn't see. It took me a while to find the turn-off button."

Mom wrapped her arms around him and squeezed. "I guess I'm going to have to give you some cooking lessons, kiddo." She blew out a puff of air, then glanced at me. "Leilani, why don't you wash up? You're nearly as grimy as Kimo."

"Sure." I turned and marched toward my bathroom.

She hollered. "And be careful with your left arm."

I heard Mom dragging Kimo to the big bathroom off the hallway. "Take off those clothes and I'll bring you some fresh ones." The door shut and Mom yelled, "And clean yourself really well or I'm going to throw you in the tub."

Grinning, I imagined Kimo cringing while grabbing a washcloth and scrubbing every inch of his scrawny body. He hated the ocean, swimming and even the bath. Where did he get that anyway? I loved everything water-related. Maybe he wasn't really my brother. Perfect answer to why he irritated me so much.

It took me longer than normal since I could only use my right hand, but I finished washing my face and legs. I also picked out some leaves, mashed pineapple and dirt from my hair. Staring at myself in the mirror, I filled my cheeks with air. My arms were going to be a problem. I released the pent-up breath and turned on the faucet. Drenching both arms under the running water, I watched as the sticky grime swirled its way down the drain.

I shut off the flow, grabbed a towel and dried as best as I could with my right hand. Pain shot through my left arm and wrist. Holding it close to my chest, I headed to the kitchen for some ice.

Mom was busy wiping down the fridge. "Hey, Mom, can I get some ice?"

"Oh, I'm so sorry." She turned and tossed the cloth into the sink. "I'm such a terrible parent, worrying more about the kitchen mess than my daughter's injury."

No, Mom was pretty great — not perfect, but pretty great anyway. "I'm okay." 'Course, there was the whole Kimo thing. She always sided with him, and it frustrated me.

She dug in the freezer and placed a handful of cubes in a bag. She stepped close, wrapped her arms around me and drew my cheek into her shoulder. "Don't want to hurt your arm." She barely squeezed. "I love you."

Maybe she wasn't as mad as I thought, but I still had to figure out how to convince her to make it to the potluck. "Love you, too, Mom."

Smiling, she released her hug, then dangled the ice bag in front of me. "Here you go, sweetie. Be sure to wrap it before putting it against your skin."

I nodded, grabbed some paper towels and made my way to the sofa.

Plodding down the hall past the bathroom, she yelled, "Kimo, let's go."

"Coming." He galloped into the living room and stopped short in front of me. "Told you you'd be in trouble."

"Don't you wish. I only had a little accident." I shifted the ice pack and glared at my brother. "Just so you know, this was your fault."

"Uh-uhhh."

I nodded. "Yup. You following me and yelling at me made me trip. And now I probably have a broken arm."

Kimo screamed in his shrill little voice. "Mahhhhm! Leilani's being mean."

Mom appeared, and grabbed her purse and keys. "Will you two please stop bickering?" She wagged a finger toward the door. "Get your slippers and let's go."

Kimo grabbed his flip-flops and bounded outside, but not before turning and sticking out his tongue.

Cute.

*****

Silence blanketed our trip to the clinic. Was my fighting with Kimo ruining everything? We *had* to go to the church tonight. It was mega-important we start our investigation right away. But what if I'd broken my arm and it took forever to see the doctor, have X-rays and get a cast? How could Mom finish the cakes in time? *Think, Leilani.* Maybe she'd go without the dessert. Probably not. I had to make sure we made it to the potluck. Ideas fluttered through my mind, but I struggled to figure out which one would work.

We drove through the parking lot and found a perfect spot for the gigantic SUV. Mom took the key from the ignition, flopped backward into the seat and sighed. "Ahh. So nice."

I glanced at Kimo sitting in the back. He stared at me with Frisbee-sized eyes. I shrugged. "What's nice?"

Mom chuckled and turned her head. "The break from you two fighting." She leaned over and grabbed her purse. "Come on. Let's get in there and see about your arm."

Lowering myself from the truck, I settled on one of the ideas. It could solve the whole guava disaster and get us to the church dinner.

Kimo skipped up from behind and danced around me, distracting me from the mission in my head. "Can I be the first to sign your cast?"

"Don't know if I'll have one." I moved toward the clinic, Kimo still galloping.

"I think casts with all sorts of things drawn and written on them are so cool. I really want to write on yours, okay?"

"Yeah, well, maybe you should write, 'Dork Boy, Kimo, who caused this.' Then I'll let you sign it."

"Mahhhhhhhhm!" Kimo put on his best whine and puppy-dog eyes.

Mom grabbed Kimo's arm and pulled him to the opposite side. "I knew the silence was too good to be true." She shook her head, marched through the automatic door and to the front counter.

I glanced at the walls and furniture around me. The clinic wasn't as cold feeling as the hospital, but the same gross smell bothered me.

The receptionist, wearing a name tag with *Maggie* written on it, looked up and smiled. "May I help you?"

Mom dug in her purse. "My daughter took a fall and I think her arm could be broken." She produced the insurance card.

Cringing at the sound of a screaming child echoing from an exam room, I prayed. *Please, Lord, I don't want a shot.* I could take a big-time surfing wipeout or a wakeboard face-plant, but *needles?* A shiver crept up my spine.

Maggie snatched the medical card, gazed at the giant computer screen and began typing. "I see Dr. Lim is her primary care physician." She tapped some more. "Go ahead and take a seat. You're lucky. Today's been slow, so it won't be long."

Yes! Great news to help operation get-to-the-potluck. Now if I could only pull off the rest. But it meant I needed to convince Mom to help.

We moved to a corner of the waiting area. Kimo headed straight for the magnet table and began pulling the little metal balls through the maze. I sat and eyed the magazines. Nothing good. It seemed, whenever I had to wait somewhere, the only stuff to read was about fishing, cars, health or national news. How boring was that?

Sighing, I plopped backward onto the soft sofa. Very stupid. The movement jarred my tender arm. Even the ice didn't help.

I ignored the throbbing and fixed my gaze on the approaching nurse. "Leilani Akamai?"

"Yes." I stood and sent a smile in her direction.

"The doctor can see you now."

Mom placed a hand on Kimo's shoulder. "Let's go."

Eyes still fixed on the maze, he seemed to ignore her.

The nurse smiled. "It's okay. He can stay out here." She nodded toward the receptionist. "Maggie will keep an eye on him."

"You bet." Maggie grinned. "I think the magnet table is really fun too."

He nodded, but didn't look up.

Mom tousled his hair. "Kimo, you wait here and don't get into any trouble."

I doubted Kimo even knew what it meant to not get into trouble. Mom and I headed to the exam room where she helped hoist me onto the table. I didn't have time to talk to her about the potluck or to think about the pineapple criminals before Dr. Lim walked in.

He looked up from his clipboard. "Leilani, looks like you have a little problem, huh?"

"I won't have to get a shot, will I?"

"Whoa! I think you're on fast-forward. Let's rewind a bit. Why don't we take a look at your arm?" He set his clipboard on the counter.

I removed the ice pack.

Dr. Lim fingered the area. Adjusting his glasses, he leaned in for a closer look. "Hmm. We need to X-ray the arm, but I'm guessing you broke it right above your left wrist." He moved to the counter, made notes and pointed. "Go right. You'll see the sign for X-ray. I'll meet you back here." He left the room.

Mom helped me slide off the table, and we trekked down the hallway to Radiology.

I followed the technician's directions. Why would they have you twist your arm at such weird angles when you're in pain? I was glad when he removed the heavy apron and sent me back to the exam room.

While we waited for Dr. Lim to bring in the verdict, I decided to test my plan with Mom. "I have an idea."

"Oh, yeah?"

Words spilled from my mouth like a thundering waterfall. "If I have to get a cast, why don't you go home so you can finish the guava cakes? You could pick me up when I'm done. Then we can go tonight."

"Sweetie, I don't think there's enough batter left to make both cakes."

"Can't you make just one instead of two? No one's going to care if you only bring one."

Mom moved close and leaned on the table. "I still don't get what's so important about you going to the church dinner."

I sighed. "I already told you. Maile, Sam and I want to hang out."

"Hmm. Must be something mighty important you three plan on discussing." She grinned and leaned even closer. "Boys, maybe? Or are you and Maile trying to hook Sam up with one of your friends again?" She shook her head. "Poor guy."

Mom gave me the perfect out. I hung my head, twisted my mouth and spoke softly. "Yeah, you're right." Now maybe she'd go home and bake. "Don't tell Kimo, okay? He'll drive me crazy tonight." And every day for the rest of my life.

"Well, Miss Leilani." Dr. Lim paraded in, waving an X-ray. "Looks like you have yourself a nice big break in that arm of yours." He held it up to the light, pushed his glasses higher on the bridge of his nose and pointed with a pencil. "See there?"

"Yeah."

"That's the fracture."

"What's all the dark stuff around it?"

"Blood."

"Yuck!"

Dr. Lim grabbed his clipboard and made more notes. "You need to go to the cast room."

"Can my mom go home for a while and come back later?"

He looked up from the chart. "Certainly." He pointed his pen in Mom's direction. "Be sure to check in with Maggie before you leave. She'll have some paperwork for you to sign."

I grinned at Mom.

She shook her head and passed me a lopsided smile. "Okay. I'll finish up the baking."

"Cool."

She patted my leg, snatched her purse and left the room.

Dr. Lim turned pages in my medical file. "Hmm. One more thing, Leilani. Looks like you're not up-to-date."

"What do you mean?"

"You need a tetanus shot."

Ehā
(Four)

Good grief! What a ridiculous day. How much worse could it get? At least Dr. Lim sent in the nurse to give me the shot before I headed to the cast room. Less time to anticipate the needle.

I survived the ordeal and now sat amongst rolls of plaster tape, a bucket of water and rubber gloves, waiting for the cast guy. Visions of Mom pulling a guava cake from the oven danced in my head. We would for sure make it to the potluck. I grinned.

A young redheaded man in a lab coat approached. "Hello, Leilani. My name is Dan. I'm going to be applying your cast today." Before I could answer, he placed his hands on my arm and lifted, resting the throbbing thing upright on my elbow. "I need you to hold your arm in this position."

I grimaced.

"I know it can be painful, but once this bad-boy cast is on, you'll feel a whole lot better."

"Okay. I believe you."

He chuckled, slipped my arm into a little stocking thing with a hole for my thumb and held up a roll of white tape. "This is the padding I'll apply before the plaster rolls." He wrapped it in a spiral around my arm.

Fascinated, I watched him work. After he finished the soft layer, he dunked a powdery plaster roll in the bucket of water, squeezed, shook and coiled. He stayed silent, and I appreciated the quiet time to think.

Notes and ideas flowed through my head. I'd write them down later.

First, fill Sam in on the crime.

Second, make a list of suspects and motives.

Third, plan how and when to interrogate — oops! — *interview* those suspects.

I glanced at my arm. The plaster creation grew in length and thickness as Dan applied more and more of the goopy mesh rolls.

"Are you ready for the fun part?" He dipped his hands in the pan of water.

"Bring it on, Dan-The-Cast-Man." I twisted my mouth into a silly grin.

He winked and wiped his wet palms over the layers, smoothing the gunk.

I loved the sensation as the plaster warmed. I shoved away the desire to float off into daydreams. Where was I, on my list? Oh, yeah...

Fourth, plan a stakeout in the pineapple fields.

Fifth, find a connection to the Tong Plantation and its workers.

Number five seemed the most difficult. Maybe Maile or Sam knew someone who worked there. We could interview that person. Or maybe there was someone else who could introduce us to a staff person. Maybe our moms had a connection to a plantation employee.

I grinned at my perfect plan. Now if I could only remember my ideas long enough to record them.

"I'm glad to see you're smiling." The technician squeezed and pressed all over the cast. When he was done, Dan wiped white splatters off my fingers and upper arm. "This must be hard for you, having this cumbersome thing in the summer."

"Yeah."

"We'll let the plaster set up for a few more minutes." He patted his handiwork and winked. "Hope you're not a surfer, 'cause your career will have to wait a while."

I sighed. "Yup, I am." Of course I surfed…and wakeboarded, windsurfed, boogieboarded and snorkeled.

"Sorry."

"It's a bummer, but I'll find something else to keep me busy." I squeezed my lips tight — like detective work and tracking down a criminal.

Dan checked my arm-prison one more time, then wrapped it in a sling and helped me down. "You can take the sling off later if your arm's feeling better."

"Thanks. I'll recommend you to all my friends with broken arms or legs."

He chuckled as I shuffled down the hall to the lobby. I headed to the closest chair and settled in. Digging for my cell, I smiled. Pushing the numbers with my exposed left fingers wouldn't be a problem, but I decided to let my arm rest in its cloth cradle. I was talented in one-handed dialing. After punching in the number, I waited for my mom's voice.

"Hello."

"Kimo, where's Mom?"

"She's frosting the guava cake."

Yes! We were going to make it to the church potluck. "Can you tell her I'm ready to come home?"

"Did you get a big cast?"

"Yeah –"

"How long is it?"

"Not ver –"

"Can you move your fingers?"

"Of cour –"

"Can I sign it?"

It was silly to even try to answer Kimo's questions. He plowed over my words like an out-of-control wave at Pipeline.

"Leilani? Can I sign it, puleeeeeeze?"

"Maybe. Now will you just get Mom?"

"You can't talk to her until you say yes."

I clenched my teeth. My little pain-in-the-pants brother was about to make me scream. I heaved out a blast of air. "Fine."

"Yaaaaaaaaay!" I heard Kimo's feet pounding the ground, and imagined him dancing around in circles. "Here, Mom. It's Leilani, and she said I can sign her cast first, before anyone else."

I hollered. "Not what I said, nerd-boy." No use, Kimo couldn't hear me over his whooping.

"Hi, sweetie. You ready?"

"Yup."

"I'll be there in a few minutes."

I hung up, groaned and planned to strangle my little brother. Before I could figure out how to get away with it, though, my phone buzzed — Maile's home number. Visions of her cell in a b'zillion pieces danced through my mind. "Hey!"

"Hi, Leilani. How's your arm?"

"Broken. I have a cast."

"Cool. Can't wait to sign it tonight. I'll be the first, okay? Oh — wait — are you coming?"

I sat up straight and grinned. "Yup. Mom finished the cake."

"Good. Sam's coming too. He's just like you — super excited about investigating a real crime."

"I think I'll give him a call."

"Okay. See you tonight."

A giggle bubbled in my throat. How great was this? Looked like my day would end in perfection, or at least better.

I clicked on the favorites button for Sam's house. Squirming, I wondered what ideas Sam Bennett would have. He'd been my best bud since kindergarten when we'd played in the sand with little buckets and shovels. He was the most creative of our group. But that was when it was just Detective Club pretend. Hoped he'd be as good with a real crime.

"Leilani! Knew it was you. You okay? Duh, of course you are since you're on the phone. Heard about your trip. Ha! Ha! Funny, huh?"

I chuckled. Sam could rival my brother in the fast-talking department. "I'm fine."

"Cool, 'cause I'm on this whole pineapple thing. Did you make notes and stuff?"

"Not yet. I've been a little busy at the doctor."

"Oh, man. Duhhhhh." His laugh blasted through the phone, punctuated with a snort. "I'll write down some ideas too."

"Good. Exactly what I wanted to ask you to do. Be sure to be crazy creative, okay?"

"No pro-blem-o! Hey — your mom bringing guava cake? My mom's making coconut cookies. Tried to test one out, but she slapped my hand, said I could make my own and eat as many as I wanted. Told her I would, but wouldn't wear a dorky apron." He bellowed so loud that my eardrum ached. "Can you see that? Me in a stupid girl's apron, waving a wooden spoon in the air?" He hooted and added a snort. "Totally gross-city. Anyway, I want to be the first to sign your cast. Promise I won't scribble. You got one, right?"

"Yeah, I got a cast. Yes, Mom's bringing a guava cake. And I love anything with coconut. So, see you tonight." I licked my lips at the thought of Mrs. Bennett's yummy cookies.

"Way cool!" His words garbled. Probably stuck some kind of food in his mouth. "Don't tell anyone, but I've kinda missed the whole Hawaiian Island Detective Club thing." He burped and I pulled the phone from my ear. Sam was my friend, but he could really gross me out sometimes. "A real mystery, huh? I'm totally in. Bring it on, Leilani! Bye."

I pocketed my phone and stood. A gigantic smile overtook my face. In spite of my stupid broken arm, this summer was going to be amazing. With my detective skills, Maile's common sense and Sam's creativity, we would crack this pineapple case wide open. This could be the start of a whole detective career for me. I sighed. Could my thoughts possibly sound any dorkier?

I sauntered toward the entry, expecting Mom to pull in any minute. I gazed out the huge windows and wondered how to choose between Maile and Sam. Both wanted to be the first to sign my cast. Maybe they could sign it at the same time.

A horn honk interrupted my thoughts. I waved at my mom, then headed out the door.

She rolled down the window. "Hey, sweetie. How's the arm feeling?"

"Much better." I struggled to boost myself onto the running board and into the SUV. "But now my right one hurts."

She pulled out of the lot and headed toward home. "Why? What happened?"

"Dr. Lim and the notes in his stupid chart happened."

Mom scrunched her nose and cocked her head.

"Why does he have to be so picky about getting everything right, anyway?"

"I don't understand. Isn't that a good thing?"

"Nope. Not when it involves needles."

"Ohh." She nodded. "Tetanus shot. They caught me right before I left the office to get permission."

I cringed. "And the stupid thing hurt big-time."

"I know. Sorry, Leilani, but it's good you got one. Never know what may have poked you when you fell."

"Yeah, I guess. I do have a lot of cuts and stuff."

"I hope you're happy about going to the potluck tonight. I got the cake done."

"Thanks, Mom. You're the greatest."

"I guess I owe you a thank-you for sending me home." She slipped me a sideways glance and a smile. "I hated to miss the potluck as much as you, and the cake turned out great."

Pleased with my clever plan to get us to the church, I smiled. The only thing I still hoped for was seeing Kainoa at the dinner. But what if he brought Carly? Clenching my teeth, I prayed the ugly visions would die a quick death.

Without warning, my body lurched forward and then my head jerked backward. The seatbelt grabbed my shoulders and tightened. Gravel and dust exploded all around the truck. A blurry vision of another vehicle crossing in front appeared through the dirt haze. The noise of grinding tires and high-pitched yelling echoed in my ears. Were those screams coming from me?

We stopped. I coughed and fanned away the dust. My whole body shook. I turned my head and stared at my mom.

Her head and limp hands rested on the steering wheel. She didn't move.

Elima
(Five)

"Mom?" My one good hand fought the seatbelt until it finally unlatched. I leaned toward her and battled the queasiness bubbling in my stomach.

She groaned and lifted her head off the steering wheel. "Oh my…"

I gulped and touched her arm. "You okay?"

"Yeah." She ran a hand across her forehead and exhaled. "Just a little rattled."

A 20-something man in baggy jeans piled out from an old blue pick-up and jogged to the driver's side of our car. He bent, leaned against the side and poked his head through the open window. "I'm so sorry. You two alright?"

Mom nodded.

He handed her a business card. "My name is Brody Trent." Despite the dusty cloud around him, his blue eyes sparkled. His short, cropped hair, covered with dirt, looked lighter than it probably was. Low and soft, his voice comforted. "Your quick reaction saved us both a lot of headaches."

"Uh-huh, not to mention the hassle with insurance companies." Her lips curved.

Relief flooded my insides.

She tucked renegade strands of hair behind her ears. "What happened, anyway? Where did you come from?"

"The side road." A slight smile crept across his lips as he shook his head. "I'm not a reckless driver, but every once in a while the brakes on that old thing act up. I'm so sorry. The old contraption of a vehicle just kind of decided to whip across the main road and ignore my shoving on the pedal."

"You should get it fixed." My mom focused her stare on his eyes and frowned. "Next time you might hurt somebody."

"Yeah, well, it's a company truck and the owner is struggling a bit these days." Grimacing, he ran a hand through his grubby hair. "But you're right. I'm so sorry to have shaken you up. I'll make sure something like this doesn't happen again." Brody grabbed the edge of the window and straightened. "Please call me if I can do anything for you two." He backed away, waved and lumbered toward the worn-out truck.

"Did you hit your head, Mom?"

"No. I think anxiety and shock got the best of me and I just collapsed for a few seconds." She turned, touched my arm and smiled. "Sorry I scared you." She chuckled. "I bet I know what you're worried about. It's the potluck, right?"

"No way!"

She touched my knee. "I know. Just thought I'd use a little humor to cut the tension."

I grabbed a deep breath and settled onto the seat. Mom was okay.

She watched as Brody started his truck, backed up and stopped along the side of the road. "All's clear. Let's get you home." She put the car in gear and glanced in my direction. "Don't forget to buckle up."

As we pulled away, I took a closer look at his vehicle. It had writing on the side. Peeling paint, dents and rust made it hard to read the letters. I squinted and tried to decipher.

ONG   P N A ON

Most of the letters seemed to be missing, but a name popped into my mind. Could it be *Tong Plantation?* Or maybe I just imagined it because of the article, the crime and our meeting tonight. No, it fit. Couldn't be anything else.

Yes! I shimmied in my seat. Couldn't wait to tell Maile and Sam.

We zoomed by towering palms, their fronds swaying in the gentle breeze. I breathed in the tropical scents of sweet flowers and salty ocean.

Mom turned and drove a few more blocks to our house. "Leilani, could you please get your brother? I'll pack up the cake."

Oh, man. I'd have to deal with Kimo. "Okay."

"Meet you two back at the car."

I unloaded my battered body, trudged my way into the house and kicked off my flip-flops. The house smelled like heavenly guava cake. I took in a lungful of the sugary smell and licked my lips as if I could actually taste the dessert. The aroma lingered, even down the hall toward my little brother's room.

Raising my hand, I prepared to knock on Kimo's door, but before I could, it flung open and Kimo's gangly legs propelled him up and down. "You're back!" His smile stretched across his face. "Can I see the cast? Puleeeeeeeeeze? Can I? Can I?"

"Cool it." I glued the sling tight against my chest. "I'll let you see, but first you have to get your clothes changed and brush your teeth, okay?"

"'kay."

"I'll meet you by our slippers out front."

Kimo nodded and made a run for the bathroom.

I ducked into my room and rummaged through a stack of books, papers and spiral notebooks. I finally located an unused one and pulled it from under the pile. The entire mound rumbled to the floor like lava down a mountain. Great. Another mess to clean up. It would have to wait. Grabbing a pencil, I hoped for a more successful evening with my friends.

I made my way to the front door, put on my flip-flops and waited for Kimo. Before I could click the mechanical pencil and make some notes, he skipped across the room, singing in full voice and performing all the hula motions.

"Oh, we're going to the hukilau. Huki, huki, huki, huki, huki, hukilau."

After he reached me, Kimo slipped on his flip-flops and waved a gold metallic Sharpie in my face. He continued to sing to the tune. "Oh, I'm gonna sign my sister's cast. Sister, sister, sister, sister, sister, sister's cast."

Chuckling, I shook my head. Sometimes I wished I could be ten years old again, never caring about how silly I looked or how crazy I sounded. But being 13 meant I had to grow up and act more like an adult. I liked it, but sometimes being older was hard.

"Okay, here you go." I took off the sling and tossed it on the couch. "Sign away." One problem solved. I wouldn't have to choose between Maile and Sam to be the first to autograph my cast.

Kimo wrinkled his nose and stuck it close to whatever he was writing.

"Hurry up. Mom's waiting."

He ignored my command and continued his work. After a couple more strokes, he pulled his head back and snickered.

"Ta dah!"

I cocked my head, trying to get a right-side-up look at his masterpiece. "Ha, ha, you little rat."

My brother, the artist, burst into a full belly laugh.

I bit my lip to thwart a grin. Didn't want Kimo to think I thought it was hilarious. His wobbly signature shined gold under a picture of a head. A squished pineapple dripped down the face and the fruit's spiky crown sat on top.

"See? It's how you broke your arm. Isn't it funny?"

"I didn't look like that." Shaking my head, I grabbed his arm. "Let's go." Kimo surprised me with his amazing artistic talent. No matter what he drew, I could recognize it because he added great details, even if the sketch wasn't perfect. Someday he'd make it big, for sure.

We headed outside. Mom sat behind the steering wheel of the SUV, motioning for us to hurry.

Kimo and I piled in, and we headed out. "No accidents on the way, okay, Mom?"

*****

The church buzzed with voices and movement, and I dodged people, tables and chairs while looking for my two friends. I swallowed hard. What if, after everything I'd been through, they didn't come?

Clutching the notebook to my chest, I panned the room. Sam — earbuds in place — performed a few hip-hop moves near the dessert table, his shaggy blonde hair flopping in time to the music. If I had as much energy as him, I could conquer every wave with no problem. Sam should take up surfing, but he was definitely more the hip-hop and martial arts type.

He unwrapped a plate of coconut cookies and dumped it next to my mom's guava cake.

"Hey, Sam!"

My friend spotted me and stuck a hand in the air.

I made my way to him. "Have you seen Maile?" I reached around Sam and grabbed a cookie.

He pulled the buds from his ears and shoved them in a pocket. "Yeah. She's here somewhere." He glanced around and then focused on my arm. "Wow! You're totally casted up. Got a pen?"

"Sorry," I sighed. "Had to let Kimo write on it first."

Sam shrugged. "No pro-blem-o."

I downed the rest of the chewy treat and enjoyed every bit of the sweet coconut shreds. "Why don't we get some dinner and head to the preschool room?"

" 'kay. I'll sign your cast then."

The line for food grew longer as we headed toward it, but we managed to reach the other side of the room and beat out a swarm of hungry kids. The serving tables — loaded with main dishes and salads — stretched along an entire wall. Aromas tickled my nose every step of the way. Lomi salmon, beef teriyaki, chicken long rice, char siu bao, poi and kalua pig. The pig had cooked for hours in the Hawaiian underground pit outside. An imu was the best way to cook a whole one.

It was very tempting to overload my plate. 'Course, serving myself progressed slowly, as I had to set the plate down every time I wanted to dish up a spoonful. I turned at the tap on my shoulder. "There you are, Maile. Did you get something to eat?"

"Yup." Maile placed both hands on her hips. "Look at your arm! You doing okay with getting food?"

"Yup."

"When can I sign?"

"Later, okay? After we meet."

"My plate is over there." She pointed. "Both our moms are sitting at the table too."

"We decided to meet in the preschool room, remember?"

"Does your mom know?"

I shook my head. "Nope."

Maile squinted at me.

"Okay. I get it. I'll be over in a minute and let my mom know where we'll be."

"Good." Maile cocked her head. "I see you came prepared with your spiral." She nudged me, turned and zigzagged between tables.

I dished up a little more and stared at the mega-full plate. What made me think I could eat so much food? Sam loaded his even higher than mine. I'd seen him eat—he could handle it.

"You ready?" He dunked a piece of pork in the poi and popped it into his mouth, then garbled his words through the half-chewed food. "Man, this is good."

I nodded. "Let's go."

We made our way to the table. I took a moment to glance around the room. No Kainoa. Was he with Carly? I squeezed my lips tight.

"I see you managed to load up pretty well." My mom smiled.

"Yeah. I kind of surprised myself. We're going to hang out somewhere else, okay?"

She sighed and narrowed her eyes. "Guess Luana and I will have to survive without you teens around. Whatever will we talk about?" She smiled. "Go ahead. Have fun."

I turned and headed toward the door. The preschool room

was across from the social hall. The kid-sized chairs and low tables greeted us.

Sam set his plate down, lumbered toward the bulletin board and stared at the bright-colored artwork. "I kinda miss preschool."

"For real?" Maile plopped onto a chair.

"Yeah. Don't you remember how fun it was to play all day? Now school is such a drag." He shoved his hands into his board-short pockets. "Sure glad it's summer."

I joined Maile, dropped my notebook onto the table and settled in. "Yeah, games and stuff like the detective club were fun and all, but now we get to investigate for real and solve a crime." I jiggled with excitement and shoveled in a huge bite.

Maile tore off a piece of char siu bao. "Speaking of detective things, let's see what notes you scribbled." She chomped on the pork-filled bun.

Sam trudged over and sat with us. "Yup. Whachya got, Leilani?" He picked up his fork and dug into the rice and teriyaki beef.

I opened the spiral and read the plan out loud. In between each item on the list, I paused and devoured the yummy dishes in front of me. Everything tasted so good, especially the pork. All the dads had helped cook it. Maile and Sam's dads were at the church early in the morning to dig the hole for the Hawaiian underground bar-b-que pit, and prepare the pig to cook in the imu.

Usually I loved being a team with Mom and Kimo since Dad died. I'd been doing a great job of ignoring the ache and emptiness, but then I tasted the pork. Sadness poured over me like a crashing wave. Dad had been the head pig-and-imu guy for years. He loved it.

"Your plan sounds cool," Maile shifted in her seat, "but where do we start?"

I rubbed my head. Thoughts shot through my brain, but nothing seemed right. "I don't know." Suddenly a picture flashed in my mind — the Tong Plantation truck. I sat upright and opened my eyes wide. "I figured out the most difficult part of the plan."

My friends stopped mid-chew.

"This is so amazing." I waved my hand to emphasize each word. "We have a contact at the Tong Plantation."

Sam looked at me, his mouth gaping. "Huh?"

"Yeah. Today my mom's SUV was almost hit by one of the trucks from the pineapple fields. We met the guy who was driving. His name is Brody Trent, and I'm sure he'd talk to us if we contacted him."

"Cool." Sam's mouth listed to one side. "I mean, not cool about your mom almost having an accident."

Maile giggled. "We know what you mean."

"Do you think both of you can meet tomorrow if I call him?"

"Sure." Maile nodded.

Sam burped. Was belching a sport? Sam could make it to the Olympics for sure. "I'm not busy." Then he shoveled in his last bite of rice and beef teriyaki.

"Great." I gathered up my plate, fork and notebook.

We moved toward the door when I heard it — some blocks in the play area crashed to the ground.

Maile and Sam stopped and stared at me.

Somebody was in the room, and whoever it was had heard our entire plan.

Eono
(Six)

I stood on tiptoes and tried to peer over the storage shelves. A pile of jumbled blocks came into view, along with a familiar flip-flop. "Kimo?"

He crawled out and stared at me.

Hands planted on my hips, I glared molten lava at my brother. "What are you doing in here?"

Kimo stood and shrugged. "I heard you talking to Maile about meeting here, so I came in first and hid over there." He grinned. "I'm a pretty great detective, huh?"

"You got caught, ding-dong."

"Yeah…" Kimo scrunched his face and tucked both hands into his pockets. "Well, I still think I'm good, and you should let me into the Hawaiian Island Detective Club."

I marched over and gripped his skinny arm. "You'll have to start your own, 'cause we're not doing that anymore. It's baby stuff." I dragged him out the door. Maile and Sam followed behind.

"Leilani, I can walk by myself. You don't have to pull me." Kimo squirmed. "So what were you guys talking about in there?"

I ignored his question and trucked toward Mom. She could deal with my annoying little brother.

"Hey! You were talking about a real mystery, right? You think you guys can be real detectives." He howled. "That's soooooo funny. You and Maile are girls. How can you solve a case? You need the help of a man like me."

"You're not a man. You're a twerp."

My brother tried prying my fingers to loosen my grip. "Am not. I could help you."

"Besides, we have Sam too. He's smart and way cool."

"But he's not a man either." Kimo dragged his feet against my pulling, his voice squealing higher with each step.

"He's closer to being a man than you." I glared at him. "I thought you liked Sam."

"I do, but you have two girls in the club. You need two boys too."

"Do not." A few more steps and we reached the table where Mom chatted with Mrs. O. "Mom, will you please keep Kimo with you? He was spying on us."

She focused on him, eyes as round as her hoop earrings. "Oh, Kimo. What were you thinking? Why do you always dig yourself in deeper and deeper?"

"I just wanted to help."

I frowned and folded my right arm across my cast. "Yeah. Like you tried to help make the cake?"

Kimo stuck his tongue out at me.

I scowled, shook my head and drew my face close to his.

"Okay. Enough." Mom stood up, then ushered Kimo to a chair. "You stay here." She turned and shooed me away. "And you go off with your friends and have some dessert. We'll be leaving in about 20 minutes."

I turned around and tromped toward the sweets. Maybe something yummy would tame my anger.

Maile trotted along while Sam lagged behind.

"What are we going to do about Kimo?" Maile picked up a fork and napkin. "Do you think he's figured anything out?"

I shook my head and eyed the guava cake. Balancing a plate on my cast and anchoring it with my fingers, I dug into the pink delight.

Sam charged up next to me, grabbed the knife and cut a piece.

Maile swatted him. "Hey, rude-boy. I was here first."

He ignored her. "No worries about Kimo. Your mom won't believe him. His imagination is crazy weird." Sam obviously couldn't wait until we sat before he shoved in a bite of dessert. Then he talked with his mouth full of crumbs. "She'll figure he's exaggerating or maybe even making it up." He swallowed. Thank goodness, 'cause the slobbery food in his mouth was grossing me out. "But we need to pump out a plan for this whole pineapple thing." Sam handed the knife to Maile.

After shooting Sam some foul face and loading a slice on her plate, Maile moved toward an empty table. "Let's sit here."

I sighed and plopped down on a chair. Shoving in a bite, I glanced around the room. People were still serving themselves food, probably seconds. Scanning the cakes and cookies, I spotted the two people I didn't want to see, or at least not together. I blew out a puff of air and clenched my teeth.

Kainoa stood in front of the desserts while Carly slithered along the table's edge. I gulped my cake and stared. She made her way to Kainoa's side and nestled the side of her face into his shoulder.

I wanted to throw up.

*****

At home, I lumbered into my room and fell backward onto the bed. Why did I eat that guava cake and all those coconut cookies? The remains sat in my stomach like a brick. I knew there was a reason why I didn't like potlucks. Groaning, I reached for the notebook and reviewed my scribbles.

Before writing a word, I closed my eyes and hoped to see images of a solution to the crime. But only visions of Kainoa and Carly played like a movie. I sat up and shook my head. Time to get off my bed and do something about the pineapple vandalism case. Marching out the door and down the hallway, I clenched my teeth and willed the irritating pictures in my brain to go away. "Mom?"

She popped out of the kitchen, a dishwasher basket of clean silverware in her hands.

"Do you have the card from that Brody-something guy?"

"The guy in the truck?"

I nodded.

"It's on the coffee table in the living room." I could hear her tossing silverware into a drawer as she hollered from the kitchen. "What do you need it for?"

"Nothing, really."

"Well, don't lose it."

"I won't. Thanks." I hurried to my room and plopped onto my big, cushy chair. The card had choices — office, home, cell and fax. I figured he'd be at home tonight. Punching the numbers into my phone, I contemplated what to say to Mr. Trent.

He answered after one ring.

"Mr. Trent, my name is Leilani Akamai. Don't know if you remember me, but you and my mom almost got into a car accident this afternoon."

"Oh, yes. Are you okay? Is something wrong?"

I shook my head. Silly. He couldn't see me through the phone. "No, no, nothing like that, Mr. Trent. I wanted to ask if you'd be willing to meet with me and two of my friends."

"Only if you tell me what it's about." He chuckled. "And stop being so formal. Call me Brody."

"No problem." I shifted my sitting position. "So, my friends and I want to talk with you about the vandalism in the pineapple fields."

Silence.

"Brody?"

He sighed into the phone. "Do you know something about the teens who did the damage?"

"No. I mean, it may not even be kids."

"Hmm. You're very right. And, yes, I can meet with the three of you tomorrow if you'd like."

"Great! What time?"

"How about 10:30? I have a break every morning at that time."

Balancing the spiral on my knees, I scribbled the time: 10:30. "Where do we meet you?"

"Can you and your friends make it to the plantation office? It's toward the ocean side of the fields, back away from the road."

"Oh, yeah. I've seen it before. Thanks, Brody."

A giggle overloaded with excitement escaped my throat. I clicked off my cell and tossed it on the nightstand. Our first interroga — interview. Man! I'd better not mess up tomorrow. Grabbing my phone again, I thought about how we would get to our meeting. I punched one of the quick-dial buttons. When Maile didn't answer after a couple rings, I disconnected. *Duh! She destroyed her phone earlier today.* I searched my contact list for her home number.

Mrs. O answered after two rings, and then took the phone to Maile.

"Hey, Leilani. That was fast. Did you already talk with the pineapple guy?"

"Yup. And we're meeting him at the plantation office tomorrow at 10:30."

"Very cool!"

"I've been trying to figure out how to get there. Any ideas?"

"Isn't it the building near Sam's house?"

"Yeah. We could meet there, huh?" My lips twisted to one side. "That way no one will know what we're really doing."

"Very clever, Leilani. You call Sam and we'll both make sure our moms can get us to his house."

"Sounds good."

"Oh, and don't let Kimo know anything." Maile chuckled. "We don't need your little brother popping out from behind a file cabinet or something."

I scowled. "For sure. I'll see you tomorrow."

After I pushed the quick-dial button, Sam answered. I explained the idea to him.

"Yup. We can meet here. You're almost as smart as me, Leilani." He gave a hoot and a snort. Then he started talking, about anything and everything.

Glad I didn't have a bunch more important stuff to tell him. I'd never have gotten a word in with the way he babbled on. I finally interrupted. "Okay, Sam. Maile and I will be there about 10:00 tomorrow."

"I'm pumped, aren't you? 'Course you are. This whole thing was your idea." A chuckle punctuated with another snort. "See ya."

I couldn't help but smile and shake my head. If Sam wasn't so entertaining when he babbled on and on, he'd be super annoying.

Snuggling further into the folds of my soft chair, I thought about our meeting. I grabbed the pencil and notebook. What questions should I ask? What would Brody be able to share? And if he had information, would he be willing to tell us? Or did he know anything at all? I jotted down my thoughts.

A budding yawn alerted me to how late it was, but before I could roll out of the comfy chair, my phone buzzed. I grabbed it and looked at the number — not in my address book and not anything I recognized. Shrugging, I decided to answer anyway. "Hello."

"Oh, hello, Leilani, you poor little thing. This is Carly."

Ehiku
(Seven)

Poor little thing? What was that all about? And why was Carly calling me, anyway?

"How's your arm? Kainoa told me you broke it, and I feel so terrible."

"It's fine." Why would she feel terrible? She'd never treated me like I mattered.

She giggled. "You know, now that I'm with Kainoa, I feel like you and Maile are my younger sisters, and I don't want anything bad to happen to you two cuties."

There it was again. *Cuties.* Everything inside my stomach bubbled up like Kilauea threatening to erupt. I'd been trying really hard not to think about Kainoa, and now Carly had to call and make everything horrible. I hated being 13. Why couldn't I be 16?

"Anyway, I'm sure you need to get your rest with all the excitement today, so I'll talk to you tomorrow, okay?"

Not if I could possibly avoid it. "Okay." I tried really hard to sound sweet, but every one of my words had come out like a growl. Had she noticed?

She hung up, and I threw my phone onto the bed. What I really wanted to do was whack it against the wall. I sighed. No use destroying my phone over an irritating neighbor.

When would Kainoa come to his senses about Carly? I rubbed my head. Maybe he'd never figure her out.

I stood and dug out some pajama shorts and a t-shirt from my dresser. The cast slipped easily into my shirt. After brushing and flossing, I moved to the side of my bed and knelt like I'd always done with my dad.

"Dear Lord, thank you for all your blessings. Please take care of Mom, Kimo and me." I paused and looked up from my folded hands. "Dear Lord, I miss my dad. Please help me and Kimo to be good for Mom. She misses him too."

*****

Kimo's whooping and running down the hall tore me out of Dreamland. Usually I'd yell at him, but today I was glad for the early morning wakeup call. I bounded from bed and out my door, and nearly plowed over my brother. "Watch out!"

Mom glared at me as I burst into the kitchen. "What on earth has you moving so fast this morning?"

"Can you take me to Sam's house in half an hour?"

"I suppose." She cocked her head and leveled her eyes with mine. "What's so important at Sam's house?"

"Nothing." I shrugged. "Maile's coming too. We wanted to hang out again since Kimo interrupted last night." Smiling inside, I was proud of my perfect explanation.

"Okay." She set her coffee on the island and grabbed a plastic bag. "Here. Let me help you get that cast covered so you don't get it wet when you shower."

I stretched my arm toward her. She slipped the bag over it and added two rubber bands above the white plaster.

"I fixed some pancakes this morning, so after your shower, I want you to eat."

"Mom, I want to get to Sam's. I'll just take a banana with me and eat it in the car."

Her eyes lasered right through me. "I will *not* be driving you to Sam's if you don't eat pancakes at the table this morning." She smirked. "And if you really want a banana, I'd be happy to cut one up on top of the stack."

I drew in a breath to voice a protest when I was interrupted from behind.

"Bet I know why Leilani wants to go to Sam's so fast." Kimo zipped past me and stood his ground next to Mom.

I glared at him, but I really wanted to strangle him.

"They're going to try to solve a mystery." He beamed as if he'd just won the battle and conquered the kingdom.

Mom grinned and winked at me. "Oh, really? So you're telling me the Hawaiian Island Detective Club lives on?"

"Yeah, and it's for real." Kimo stuck out his chest like a proud peacock.

She tousled his hair. "Well, good for them. Now, why don't you go wash up for breakfast? We'll drop off your sister and then you and I can head to the grocery store."

Kimo's I'm-so-cool expression faded. "Aw, Mom. That's no fun. I want to help the girls and Sam."

"Mom!"

She waved me off and focused on Kimo. "Let your sister and her friends have their club fun." She wrapped an arm around his shoulder. "How about we have some pancakes." Then she redirected his attention to the tall can sitting on the counter. "See? I even bought squirty whipped cream. And maybe there's chocolate syrup…"

Mom's voice faded as I trekked down the hall to my shower.

I was glad she figured what Kimo told her was all part of our imaginary sleuthing.

Dropping clothes through my room on my way to the bathroom, I climbed into the shower and stuck my arm outside the curtain. The steam penetrated my skin and snaked up my nostrils. It warmed and soothed. Suds spiraling down the drain reminded me that time was slipping away too.

I dried and dressed in record time, despite my cast, then made my way to the stack of pancakes waiting on the table. "Looks great, Mom." She had added whipped cream, bananas and some chocolate sprinkles on top. My brother liked chocolate syrup, but I loved crunchies.

Kimo was almost done with his meal. White topping encircled his lips and chocolate syrup dribbled from the corners of his mouth. His words garbled as he spoke through a mouthful of pancakes. "It's real yummy."

"Yuck! Swallow before you talk." I cut into the stack and glanced at Kimo, his eyes glaring. "What?"

"Mom doesn't believe me, but I heard you and your friends last night. You're going to try to figure out who's squishing all the pineapples."

I shrugged. "That's my business, not yours."

"You should let me help. I would be really, really, really good. I know lots of stuff and I promise to help you guys with everything."

"Kimo…" I narrowed my eyes and leaned close. "No."

Staring at the goopy mess on his plate, he didn't say a word.

Again, the tug on my heart. Why did I feel sorry for the little rat? He needed to back off and find his own stuff to do. I sighed, reached across the table and gave him a nudge. "Sorry. Tell you what. If something comes up where we can use your help, I'll let you know, okay?"

He lifted his head and a tiny glint shined in his eyes. "Promise?"

"Yes." I really meant it, but I doubted there would be anything he could do to help us solve the pineapple crimes.

I shoved in multiple bites of pancake and downed the fresh mango-papaya juice.

"Okay, kids." Mom looked at her watch. "It's almost time to go. I'll meet you outside."

I gobbled the rest of my breakfast and followed Kimo down the hall.

"I'm gonna beat you to the car." He ducked into the bathroom.

"No way." I jogged into my room, brushed and swished, then dashed to the hallway.

Kimo bulleted out the bathroom door and bulldozed into me.

"You runt! I was beating you. No fair crashing into the injured competition." I ran behind him, but the wiry kid had a much easier time dodging furniture.

He swooped down and snatched his slippers in one quick motion.

Oh, man! He beat me out the door and to the car.

"I won! I won!" Kimo jumped up and down, then piled into the truck.

"That was fast." Mom started the engine while we buckled up.

The SUV rumbled down the road. I smiled, excited to be on my way to digging up the first clues. Then it hit me. I'd left the notebook on my bed.

*****

Mom backed the car out of the Bennett driveway and waved before heading down the road. I returned the hand motion and noticed Kimo in the back seat. Thumbs in his ears, he flattened his face against the window, crossed his eyes and stuck out his tongue.

I copied his contorted expression — just in time for someone opening the door to see the ugly pose. Even from behind, I must have looked totally lame. Before turning around, I prayed it wasn't one of Sam's parents.

"Uhh, what's up with the stupid look, Leilani?"

I exhaled loudly and turned. "Thank goodness it's you."

Sam leaned against the door. "Hmm. Don't want my parents to see your dorky moves, huh?"

I sneered and marched past him into the house. The Bennett home was more modern than mine, or Maile's. Huge floor-to-ceiling windows opened the main room to sunshine, breezes, and a beautiful view of the beach and ocean. Palm, plumeria, mango, banana and papaya trees filled the yard. The scents wafted through the screens, and I drew a breath of the yummy smells.

"Is Maile here yet?"

"Just called. On her way." Sam reached for a slice of papaya. "Want some?"

Grabbing my stomach, I shook my head. "No, thanks. My mom forced a huge breakfast on me this morning."

Sam motioned for me to sit on one of the bar stools. "Got any good questions?"

I rested my cast on the counter and fingered the shiny granite. Cool to the touch, it was perfect for the warm Hawaiian climate. "About that –"

A knock on the door interrupted my words.

Sam jumped down, headed to the front and opened the door.

Maile popped inside and waved. "Hey! Ready to go meet with the plantation guy?"

"Yeah." I slid off the tall stool. "I need to tell you two something."

"Okay. Well, tell us on the way." Maile grabbed my arm and pulled me outside.

Sam followed. "So, what's up?"

"I thought up a bunch of questions last night."

"Great." Maile grinned.

"Not so much. I left the notebook at home."

Sam shrugged. "No pro-blem-o." He shoved in another piece of papaya. "I'm pretty good at thinking up lots to say."

I stared at my friend. "Nawwww. Really?" Maile and I burst into laughter.

"Ha ha. You're laughing, but something I say may be the key to solving this crime."

"Know what, Sam?" I hip-bumped him. "You're probably right."

We plodded down the street. The short walk ended at the entrance to the main plantation. The large white building looked like someone's huge home. It probably was, at one time — maybe housing workers. I loved the big wraparound lanai and the palms along every side.

Sam stepped onto the porch first. "Know where we're supposed to go?"

"Brody said to ask for him."

Maile scrunched both shoulders to her ears. "I love this place. And it's so exciting."

Sam wiggled his fingers in the air. "Oh yeah, super exciting."

Maile glared at him.

"Can't wait to meet this Brody guy." Sam poked me. "What was it you said about him being *cute* or something?" He stuck a finger in his open mouth and pretended to gag.

I felt heat flood my cheeks. "Yeah, but I'm going to be professional."

We walked into the lobby and I noticed the shiny wood everywhere, — floors and moldings around the doors and along the ceilings. Big fans whirred overhead. I searched for a secretary or receptionist to help us. Before I could locate someone, loud noises distracted me.

Two men were yelling at each other.

Ewalu
(Eight)

Maile's eyes grew larger as the arguing grew louder. The voices came from one of the offices. I looked at my friends, moved in close and whispered, "Follow me. Maybe we can hear what they're yelling about." Tiptoeing across the floor, I wondered if the argument had anything to do with the trouble at the Tong Plantation.

The office door was slightly ajar. I couldn't see anything, and the words were a little muddled, but I listened.

"No! Do *not* tell me you don't know what I'm talking about. You plan on leaving the Tong Farm and taking an offer from a bigger plantation." The man's voice was deep and seemed kind of mean.

"That's not true." I wasn't sure because he hadn't said much the day before, but it was possible the voice belonged to Brody Trent.

"I heard you talking about it last week."

"What?"

"And now we've been having these mysterious vandals." The harsh voice grew angrier. "You're trying to destroy this place, aren't you?"

"No. I'd never do anything to hurt the Tong family."

The man slammed something — maybe his fist — on a desk or table. "Absolutely right, you'll never hurt them, because I'm going to stop you."

I whispered to Maile and Sam. "Let's get out of here." I pointed down the hall and we scampered as fast as we could, trying not to make a lot of noise.

The door to the office burst open, crashing against the inside wall.

I jumped. Huddling close to my friends, I watched the tall, stern-faced man in a suit stomp past us. His black shoes clicked, sending a vibration through the floor with every step. He continued his mad pace out the front door.

Maile peeked over Sam's shoulder. "He looked kind of angry, huh?"

"Sure did." I searched the area for a friendly face. "Let's see if there's someone who can show us where Brody's office is."

My friends followed as I rounded a corner. A woman behind a computer peered at me over half-glasses. "May I help you?"

"We have a meeting with Brody Trent. Could you tell us where to go?"

"Certainly. Down the corridor that way." She pointed. "It's the third office on your right."

"Thanks." I looked at my friends and raised my eyebrows before heading in the direction she pointed.

Sam marched around me and scanned the hallway. His face was taut and his jaw stern. "Is it the same office? It looks like it could be. Man, who do you think was having that fight? Of course, if it is the same room, one of them must have been Brody. Do you think he might be trying to ruin the pineapple plantation?" Shoulders stiff and mouth set tight, he took determined steps.

"Whoa, Sam!" I grabbed his arm. "Let's see if it's even Brody before we go any further."

I counted the doors as we passed. One…two…three. I sighed and looked at my friends. It was the office where we overheard the fight. "Here we are."

I knocked and Brody invited us in.

We shuffled through the door. "Hi, Brody. Remember me? I'm Leilani, and these are my friends, Maile and Sam."

"Yes, and it's nice to meet your friends." He stood and motioned toward a big table. "Come on in and take a seat."

"Thank you for meeting with us." I sat.

Brody moved his desk chair and joined our threesome.

Maile stared at the shelves. "This is a really cool office." She pointed at the books. "What are all those for?"

Of course Maile would like the books. She was super smart and loved reading.

"There's a lot of history in those. Some about the pineapple industry and some about island events from the past." He pointed. "Those over there are all sorts of agriculture books that teach us the science of growing pineapples."

"Cool!"

Brody smiled. "So, how can I help you kids?"

I squirmed in my chair and pulled at the bottom edge of my tank-top. "We wanted to ask you some questions about the pineapple vandals."

His smile faded and he leaned forward, placing both elbows on the table. "I don't know what I can tell you. Besides, why would our problems interest you?"

What should I tell him that wouldn't make us sound crazy?

Maile answered while I sat open-mouthed. "It's a school thing."

"School? It's summer." He turned his face a little and sent us a sideways stare.

"It's an assignment our teacher gave us at the end of the year." Sam to the rescue. "She thought we should do a big research project over the summer, something about politics or crime. When Leilani found the article...well, it was like...cool, a local crime that may involve kids like us. Oh! But not us. We're amazing teenagers. We want to do a great job on this to kinda wow our new teacher." He finally took a breath. "And we need your help."

Brody shook his head and wiped a hand across his brow. "Whew! I think I understood that."

As a smile spread across my face, I stole a quick glance at Sam. He was right. His mega-talking saved us. I re-focused on Brody. "Can we ask you some questions?"

"Sure. Fire away."

"The article said something about big financial implications. Was there that much damage done?"

"There was enough vandalism to cause concern. For most crops it may not be a great loss, but pineapples take about 18 months to mature. So, for every fruit destroyed, it will be at least another year and a half before one will be ready to replace it."

Maile gazed at Brody, her eyes big and round. "Wow! I didn't know that."

I cocked my head. "What about suspects. Are there any?"

Brody's eyes darted away from us. "Not that I know of."

Why wouldn't he look at us? Could it be he was thinking about the man in his office who accused him of sabotage? I squirmed and caught my lower lip in a couple of teeth. "What about an inside job? Could someone who works here have an issue with the Tong family?"

He shook his head. "No, I doubt it. Mr. Tong is a great boss. He treats all his staff very well."

"As we were arriving, I saw a man leaving your office — a tall guy in a suit. He looked kind of scary. Does he work here? 'Cause, if he does, he seems like a pretty good suspect."

Brody chuckled. "That's Nico Hanes, a businessman from town. He's the boyfriend of Mr. Tong's daughter." He sighed. "But things will change once..."

"Change? What do you mean?"

"Serena Tong is an only child and will inherit the entire plantation." He shrugged. "Nico and Serena will probably get married someday. Then, as Serena's husband, he'll run the whole operation. He came to see me because he's concerned about the incidents in the fields."

Why did I leave the spiral at home? I needed to write down these names. "Brody, do you have a pad so I could make some notes?"

"Sure. Here's a pencil too." He dug in a desk drawer and handed me a yellow-lined pad and a pencil that said *Tong Plantation* along the edge.

I scribbled down the names, then looked up and smiled at Brody. "Do you like working here?"

He nodded. "I do. It's very rewarding work and our pineapples are the best of any around."

"But couldn't you get a better job at one of the larger farms?"

Brody grinned. "Yeah, probably could." He leaned back in his chair. "But I really do like it here."

"Do you personally have any suspects in mind or some kind of motive?"

"I don't know." Brody shook his head and sighed. "I think the police probably have it right. It's kids trying to get attention or something."

"What about other motives?" I leaned forward. "Is there someone out there with a grudge against Tong Plantation?"

He cocked his head. "Hmm. I doubt it. The Tong family has always been very forthright in their business dealings. Can't imagine anyone having anything against them."

I figured we had as much information as we needed for now. "I guess that's all I have to ask you. Would it be okay if we call you again when we have more questions?"

"Certainly. Anytime. I always enjoy having a group of curious young teens come visit." Brody's eyes sparkled when he smiled. He stood and escorted us to the door.

"Bye. Thanks for helping us."

"Good luck on that school project."

I nodded and quickly turned my head. Did he see any hint of dishonesty? My face flamed hot.

Sam trucked down the hall. "That was totally cool. Good questions, Leilani. Do you think we got any clues?"

"I don't know. Maybe." I glanced at my notes and realized that I'd forgotten to return the pad and pencil. "Oh, man, I need to take these back. Go ahead outside and I'll catch up."

I sauntered toward the open office. As I drew closer, I heard Brody's voice. I stopped short. "That's good, but there's a reason I called. We've got a big problem."

Eiwa
(Nine)

What should I do, go into Brody's office or just leave? I stared at the half-open door. After a moment of quiet, he spoke again. "Yeah, sounds good. So I'll see you around 3:00 at The Coffee House."

The phone receiver clicked onto the base and I bee-lined it out of there. He probably wouldn't even miss the pad and pencil. I raced down the hall and out the door, took the front steps two at a time and prayed I wouldn't fall and break my other arm. Spotting Maile and Sam near the road, I sprinted to catch up.

Maile scrunched her face and stared at me as I slowed to a stop. "We were waiting. You didn't have to run."

"Yeah." Sam pointed. "And what's with the paper and pencil? Thought you took them back."

I panted and blew out the words. "Uh huh." Fanning my face with the pad, I swallowed. "But I overheard Brody."

"Another fight?" Sam's eyebrows peaked.

"No. He was talking on the phone and said something about there being a big problem, and then it sounded like he arranged to meet the person."

Maile's eyes grew large. "Oh, man! Do you think Brody's behind the vandalism?"

I shook my head. "I don't know what to think. But one thing's for sure, we now have two suspects."

"We do?"

"Nico and Brody." I motioned. "Let's head back to your house, Sam." My stomach churned. Brody was such a nice person, but did he have an evil side?

Sam nodded. "For sure. So now we need to figure out motives — like maybe all Brody's ooey-gooey-make-me-wanna-puke talk about the Tong family was a cover-up. Or he could be moving to another company and wants to see this one bomb big-time. 'Course, why would he unless he hated them –"

"Which means there's a deeper motive." I grinned at Sam. Figured I'd better stop him before he went on forever with theories.

Maile shook her head. "We have some mega-huge work ahead."

"Yup." I tried to scribble some ideas on the pad while we walked.

She sighed. "What's our next move?"

Silent for a few moments, I arranged the thoughts bombarding my mind. Secret motives. What were they? Who did Brody call? What was the big problem? Could it be us and our questioning?

"Leilani? You there?" Maile shoulder-nudged me. "We're almost to Sam's house."

"Sorry. I was thinking."

"About?"

The house came into view and I pointed. "Let's talk when we get there."

Sam tromped ahead. "Hey, you guys go sit on the back lanai and I'll get us something to drink."

"Thanks, Sam."

Maile and I paraded down the block, rounded Sam's house and made our way onto the lanai. We settled into chairs and I slapped the paper and pencil on the table. Closing my eyes, I soaked in the cool sea breeze. I enjoyed being this close to the beach and water, but hated the fact that the ocean sports I loved were off limits. The stupid cast was ruining everything.

"Lemonade all around." Sam set glasses and a pitcher on the table. "Hold on one second." He held up a palm, then trucked back into the house.

I poured a glass for myself and Maile.

"You guys ready for this?" Sam's voice sailed through the open door before we saw him. "Coconut cookies."

"You made these?" I looked at the plate of lopsided, odd-shaped cookies.

"Yup."

"All by yourself?"

Sam shot me a little fire from his eyes. "Told you I was gonna do it since Mom always nails me for eating too many of hers."

"Thanks. They look yummy." I snatched one. Sam was the only guy I knew who would actually take on the challenge of baking. "Love these things. Don't know how many I ate at the potluck yesterday."

Sam dragged a chair to the table and joined us. "So, what ya got, Leilani?"

I swallowed a bite. "If you two don't have any plans, I thought maybe we could go to The Coffee House in town. I'm sure that's where Brody said he'd meet whoever was on the phone."

"Cool." Sam cocked his head. "But what time does he get off work?"

"I think he said 3:00."

"We can ride bikes to town. It's not too far." He took a bite of cookie and continued with a full mouth. "Oh, wait. Can you ride a bike, Leilani?"

I stared at my cast and frowned. "I think so. I used to do a lot of one-handed riding, so I'm pretty sure I can make it. 'Course, the fingers on my left hand still work, so I could use them if I needed…maybe just for braking."

"Cool." Sam raised his hand. "High-five!"

Maile and I slapped his hand, then each other's.

We talked, laughed and devoured coconut cookies. Our plan was coming together and we had two suspects. I grinned, excited about what we might discover at The Coffee House later that day.

My cell phone buzzed in my pocket. "It's probably my mom wondering when I'm coming home." I reached for it and focused on the caller information. It wasn't a number from my contacts and I didn't recognize it. It didn't look like Carly's, thank goodness. "Hello."

"Hey! Wot's da haps, Leilani?"

Kainoa? And he wants to know what's happening?

Umi
(Ten)

"Kainoa?" I opened my mouth and struggled to say something. "Could you hold on a minute?"

I didn't wait for his answer before plastering the phone against my leg. My heart pounded in my chest and ears, but I managed a whisper. "Maile, it's your brother."

"Why would he be calling your phone?"

"I don't know. Maybe he's looking for you. What should I do?"

Sam shook his head and rolled his eyes as if in disgust. "Come on, you goof, talk to him."

I tried to formulate the perfect thing to say. "Um, what's up?" Okay, not very original, but it worked.

"Your arm okay?"

"Yeah, other than being in a cast."

"Bummer."

What was he thinking? Why was he calling?

"No mo surfin', yeah?"

I sighed. "Not for a while."

"Too bad, yeah?"

Kainoa was concerned about me and my surfing? Cool! I swallowed hard and tried to calm my fluttering heart. Praying I'd sound grown-up, I said, "I'll survive."

"So, that's why I'm calling."

My stomach churned like a blender on high speed. I held in a lemonade burp.

"Since you're out of the surfing game for now, I thought maybe Carly could borrow your board. I'm teaching her how to surf."

Carly? On my precious board? No, no, no, never! I wanted to scream. Everything around me spun, and the sour juice threatened to come up. Hands shaking, I clamped my jaw tight.

"Hey, Leilani, you there?"

"Sorry." What was I going to say? Should I tell him no, never? Or should I tell him a story — that my board was being repaired? Why couldn't Carly use Maile's board? I clenched my teeth and groaned in my head. Only one choice, unless I wanted to be a selfish jerk or a big fat liar. I squeaked out the words. "Sure, no problem."

"Cool. We'll come by later to pick it up."

Great. Now I'll have to see them together again…at my house.

I closed the cell and slipped it in a pocket. Staring straight ahead, I barely heard Maile speak.

"You okay? What did my brother want?"

Anger and frustration gurgled inside. I couldn't contain the emotion. It erupted like pent-up magma. I closed my eyes, stomped my feet, shook my head and screamed. Then, humiliated by my reaction, I leaned back hard in the chair.

"Wow!" Sam's eyebrows peaked in big arches over his round eyes. "What's going on with you?"

I drew in a lungful of air and tried to speak calmly. "I saved forever to be able to buy that longboard. Even then, my dad paid the extra. I don't want anyone to use it, especially not someone like Carly."

Maile put both hands on her hips. "Are you joking? My brother asked you to let Carly use it while you're in a cast?"

"Yup."

"I may have to have a little chat with my jerk of a brother." Maile dug in her pocket. "Oh, man. I forgot. I'm phoneless until Mom lets me get a new one," she sighed, "which may be never."

"It's okay. I trust Kainoa. He's a good teacher, so he'll make sure Carly doesn't do something stupid."

"Are you talking about *my* brother?" She grimaced.

Balancing his chair on the two back legs, Sam wagged a finger back and forth between me and Maile. "So, what's going on here? Sounds like you have a problem with Carly and Kainoa. I know she's all 'I'm so cool' and everything, but what's the big deal? Are they together or something?"

I nodded.

Sam stared at Maile as if waiting for her opinion.

She raised her hands in surrender. "Hey, I don't care who my brother gets all dreamy over." She flashed a little raised brow my way. "It's Leilani who seems to have a problem with it."

I groaned and tensed my jaw. "I just think Kainoa is too nice of a guy to be hanging around with Carly Rivers. I don't trust her."

"Whatever." Maile's lips twisted to one side as she shrugged.

Sam swallowed a bite. "It *is* kinda strange Carly's hanging out with a surfer." He delivered a burp worthy of praise among all the guys in our school, and wiped the back of his hand across his mouth. "Not the pretty-boy type she's usually with."

Maile stood. "Whatever my brother does, it's his problem." She grabbed the pitcher. "We should help Sam clean up. My mom will be by in a few minutes." She padded into the house. "Need a ride, Leilani?"

"Yeah. That'd be great." I sighed, stood and grabbed a plate. Following Maile into the kitchen, I tried to push away thoughts of Kainoa and Carly, and concentrate on the great chance to pick up clues waiting for us at The Coffee House later in the afternoon.

"You okay?"

I nodded. "I guess. Just trying to think about the case instead of…other things."

Maile took the plate from me and set it in the sink. "Well, I'm excited about the spying thing this afternoon. Can't wait to see who Brody meets."

I grinned. "Same here." The pineapple case was super important — our first. And once we solved it, everyone would know we were real detectives. I'd never figure it out, though, if I let my mind drift away from the investigation. I tucked a wandering strand of hair behind my ear and jutted my chin forward. "I think my house is closest to town. How about we meet there around 2:00?"

Sam trudged into the kitchen, cradling three glasses, napkins and spoons in his arms. "Where are we meeting at 2:00?"

"Leilani's house. Then we'll ride bikes from there."

I raised my hand and smiled. "Hey, I have an idea. Maile, do you think your mom could bring your bike?"

She shrugged. "Guess so. Can I use your phone to call her?"

"Sure." I passed her my cell. Then I turned to Sam. "We could load your bike in the car, too, and take both to my house."

Sam nodded. "Sounds good. We can get on the planning gig too."

"Yup. I'll even feed you guys lunch."

Maile handed me my phone. "No problem with hauling the bikes to your house."

Great! The afternoon expedition was coming together. Sam had loaded the dishwasher — dishes faced forward, backward, sideways and on top of each other. I wondered how they'd ever get clean. After making my way outside, I wiped up crumbs on the deck table while Maile pushed the chairs into an even circle.

I grinned at the thought of me and my friends hunkered down in a café booth near where Brody sat, listening to his every word. Who would he meet? What would they talk about? Once we picked up some juicy clues, we could move forward and finger the culprit. I chuckled inside as I read an imaginary news article about the capture of the pineapple vandals, complete with a picture of the three teen heroes.

The sound of tires hitting the rough road in front of Sam's house caught my attention. "Must be your mom."

Maile sauntered to the window and glanced outside. "Yup."

Excitement bubbled inside as I galloped out the door and down the steps. I headed toward Mrs. O to thank her for hauling the bikes, but before I reached the car door, it swung open. Out stepped Kainoa.

Umikumamakahi
(Eleven)

"Hey, Leilani, cuz!"

Cuz. Why did he have to call me that? Yeah, it was sweet and all, and it meant I was his buddy…but I didn't want to be Kainoa's pal.

"Got a bike in here." He stuck one hand in his shorts pocket and leaned against the truck. "Need to pick up another, right?"

"Yeah. Sam's." Why did Mrs. O send Kainoa? I had just shoved him out of my mind and now here he was, for real, standing in front of me. I sighed. At least Carly wasn't with him.

Sam and Maile moved in behind me.

Kainoa lumbered toward us. "Hey, Sammo, where's yours?"

Sam pointed. "At the side of the house." He trekked in that direction, Kainoa following behind.

Maile grabbed my arm. "Come on, let's get in." She guided me around to the front passenger side of the big pick-up. "You get in front."

As much as I wanted to protest, I had an equal desire to be close to Kainoa. Riding up front with him would be amazing. I squeezed my lips tight in an attempt to conquer a budding smile. Hoisting myself into the truck, I took a quick mental count of how many times I had imagined this moment…way too many.

Maile and Sam climbed in the small back section of the king-cab. I watched Kainoa through the side-view mirror as he lifted the bike above his head and loaded it into the truck bed. His muscles flexed and I felt lightheaded. Was I about to faint? I was a surfer girl, not a love-crazed teeny-bopper. I shook my head, then took one last peek at Kainoa.

"Okay. All loaded." He marched around the side, eased into the driver's seat and turned the key.

Should I say something? The quiet seemed so awkward as we drove. "Thanks for taking us to my house and for loading all the bikes." I sent him a big smile.

He shrugged. "Eh, nevah mine."

Of course it was no problem for him. He was really buff and handled the bikes like they were palm fronds instead of heavy metal contraptions. And Maile told me that since he'd gotten his license, he jumped at every opportunity to drive. I was glad he took this one. He even treated me — well, all of us — like we were real teenagers.

Kainoa rounded a corner. "I was thinking since we're going to your house, I could grab your board."

So, was this the real reason he didn't mind taking us on our little trip?

My heart pounded against my ribs. I gritted my teeth and clenched my fists. It was all because of the surfboard. And Carly.

Fine. I could handle it. I forced another smile when what I really wanted to do was sneer at him. "Sure. Sounds good."

Once we arrived, Kainoa, Maile and Sam unloaded the bikes. I wasn't much good with only one arm. I shuffled to the back of my house and stared at my bright red and white board. How many hours had I babysat the twins down the road to earn enough to buy this beauty? 'Course, I never would have been able to do it if my parents hadn't given me money for my birthday last year. Dad went with me to pick it out. My favorite color had always been red — same as his — so we agreed on this amazing surfboard right away. Even on sale, it was more money than I had, so Dad paid the rest.

"Promise I'll take good care of it."

I jumped at the sound of Kainoa's voice. "Oh. I didn't hear you walk over here."

He leveled his eyes with mine and grinned. "And as soon as you're back in the game, I'll return it."

"Cool."

Did he actually smile at me? My heart fluttered as if performing little cartwheels.

*****

My eyes lingered on the truck as it faded into the distance. After a moment, only a little puff of dust remained. I trudged toward my friends.

"So what's for lunch?" Sam bounded up the stairs.

Maile and I followed behind.

"Whatever I can fix with one hand."

He wrinkled his nose. "So, you mean we're going hungry, right?"

Maile shoved Sam. "Come on. Let's help Leilani."

Sam chattered as we made our way to the kitchen. "I'm starving. I only ate three cookies, so I'm ready for lunch. What ya got in your fridge? Any leftovers?"

"I'm sure we have some beef teriyaki and fried noodles. We can have some fruit with it." I grinned. "Pretty sure I can handle that with one arm."

Maile opened the fridge and stuck her nose in. "Hey, you have some chicken curry in here too." She yanked out several containers and set them on the counter. "There we go. Now, let's eat."

"Where's your mom and Kimo?" Maile placed a scoop of noodles on her plate.

A plump papaya oozed juice as I sliced it. I conquered the fruit with one hand, as I wanted to avoid getting my cast wet. "I think Mom took him shopping."

I handed the knife to Maile and licked my fingers. "Can you finish up with the papaya? I'd better leave her a note so she won't freak out when I'm not at Sam's."

"Sure."

I wandered to the little desk and jotted on a piece of paper. I taped it to the fridge where I knew she'd see it.

After eating, we spent more than an hour howling at pictures in my scrapbooks, talking about our favorite movie heroes and trying out crazy hairstyles. Sam wouldn't let us touch his hair, so he just watched, shook his head in disgust and made fun of us.

Maile pranced around with her hair pinned in little spikes all over her head. "I think this is the best style yet."

Sam and I rolled on the couch, laughing.

I clenched my stomach. "Stop, Maile! It hurts."

"Sorry." She pulled out the pins and her hair fell just below her shoulders. "I think it's probably time for us to go."

I looked at my cell. "Yup."

Maile jogged to the front door. "I can't believe we're doing this. I'm so excited."

I joined her. "Let's go. I want to see if I can tackle the bike ride."

Our threesome plodded to the bikes and grabbed our helmets.

"Maile, why don't you lead?" I snapped the strap under my chin.

"Sure. You should follow me so Sam can keep an eye on you from behind. We don't want to lose you somewhere on the side of the road and not know it."

"I'll do fine, no need to worry."

We headed out in order. Maile looked back over her shoulder at me. "Leilani, you're swerving everywhere."

"I'm trying to get my balance." Steering with one hand wasn't hard, but the added weight of the cast made things a little lopsided. "Almost…" I tried the brakes using both sets of fingers. Worked just fine. I steadied the bike and wheeled along smoothly.

Sam hollered from behind. "You got it!"

We bulleted down the street toward town. Maile pedaled hard, keeping us at a fast pace. Every once in a while she glanced over her shoulder. "You two still with me? I'm going to take a shortcut." She turned onto a narrow dirt road. Her tires threw bits of debris and a lot of dust, making it difficult to see her. She didn't slow the speed at all.

I coughed as the dirt slipped up my nose. This area could definitely use a little rain.

Maile turned, but then disappeared into the thick haze.

Then I saw it — Maile in the dirt on the side of the narrow road and the bike lying in the middle.

And I was heading straight toward it.

ʻUmikumamalua
(Twelve)

Squeezing the brakes with all my strength, I prayed I wouldn't crash. I needed at least one good arm to survive the summer. The front tire whipped to the left. The back tire slid around as if it was a drifting car. The bike lurched to a stop, sideways next to Maile's.

Sam's yelp echoed in my ears. I stared at his rocket-fast bike heading straight toward me. Should I drop mine and run? No time to do anything.

Sam's face scrunched as he wildly swung the front tire to one side, the back one locking and spraying dirt everywhere.

Eyes closed, I raised my cast across my face and prepared for impact. Nothing. I peeked over it, then fanned the smoky billows away.

Maile stood. "Ouch! Skinned my elbow and both knees." She wiped away dirt, avoiding the injured areas. "Wow, guys! That was way cool. You both did the exact same drifting move." She pantomimed what we looked like. "And then you slid in next to each other, perfectly lined up."

Sam and I didn't say a word.

"What?" Maile raised her hands, palms up. "I'm sorry. That nasty turn just surprised me, that's all." She picked up her bike.

"Can't believe you fell, Maile. Sam and I almost landed on top of your bike. We even could have flown over it and smacked into you."

"Sorry."

I turned my front tire. "Guess the good news is, you aren't hurt bad, and Sam and I don't have a scratch."

Sam shook his head. "Yup. We don't need any more broken arms. I really thought I was going to slam right into you, though, Leilani. Scared me big-time."

"Yeah, me too. Especially when I heard you yell." I smiled at him. "Thanks for being such a great drifter."

"Think maybe I should take up the sport?" He adjusted his helmet.

I shook my head and grimaced. "Let's go, dork."

Maile pulled her bike upright and took up the lead again. "I promise to take it a little easier."

"Good." I glanced at my cell before starting to ride. "We have plenty of time."

The remainder of our trip was smooth. Sam must have had a difficult time staying quiet for so long. He started to sing. Maile and I joined him, bellowing the awful music between giggles directed at Sam's horrible screeches. We must have sung the lyrics to at least four different TV shows. Maile and I didn't know all the words, but Sam did, although he could've used some voice lessons.

Once we hit town, the tiny café was only a couple blocks away. We parked the bikes and Maile used her cable lock to secure them around a street sign.

I checked my cell. "We have about ten minutes before Brody meets the mystery person."

"Good." Maile motioned for us to follow. "Let's get a seat."

I shook my head. "Won't work."

"Why?"

"We don't know where Brody will sit and we need to be close enough to watch and hear him and the mystery person he's meeting." I sighed. " 'Course, we'll have to be careful he doesn't see us."

Sam raised his hands. "No pro-blem-o. I got it."

I smiled — Sam's creativity to the rescue.

"Okay. So, we hit The Coffee House and get a booth way at the back. We can watch for Brody. Once he sits, we can move closer."

I nodded. "Yeah. We have a better chance of not being noticed if we're already inside. Let's try it."

Maile marched down the sidewalk toward the small café. "We have only a few minutes. Let's go."

The Coffee House was a cute place with a burgundy awning over the entrance and tiny white lights in the windows. We entered and plodded toward the back, along the line of booths located by a bank of windows. Seating ourselves in the last one, I scooted closest to the window, Sam next to me. I had the best view of the sidewalk and café entrance. If he leaned a bit, Sam had a clear view of the front counter. Maile sat across from us. She had no view of anything.

A server approached and we ordered fries.

I glanced at my cell. "Two minutes after three."

"So where are they?" Maile peeked over the back of the booth toward the entrance.

Because I sat across from her, my view was straight ahead. "Don't know."

A movement on the walkway outside caught my eye. I turned and saw Brody from behind as he walked toward the entrance.

He stopped and stared up the road. "Brody's at the front door. I think maybe he's waiting for the mystery person."

"Oh, man! I didn't even see him." Maile scooted toward the window and craned her neck to see. "Hey, there he is. And it looks like someone else is coming."

Sam squirmed, bumping my shoulder. "Man, I can't see a thing outside." He squeezed closer to me and leaned.

"Sam, move over. You'll see them when they come in." I strained to observe the other person, but Brody blocked my view. I continued to stare when Brody reached for the door with one hand and extended his arm toward his friend.

"They're inside." I stretched to see over the top of the booth and watched the mystery person enter. A woman. Don't know why I thought it had to be a man.

"Hey, it's a girl." Sam cocked his head.

They turned and headed straight toward us. I slinked down in the booth. The server arrived and placed a huge plate of fries and a bottle of ketchup in front of us. She turned and spoke to Brody and his friend, who were approaching the booth in front of ours. "Be right with you two." Then she refocused on us. "Can I bring you some water or something else to drink?"

Maile spoke in a low voice and nodded. "Water, please."

The seats in front of us squeaked as Brody and the woman slid in. She faced our booth, so if I rose up a bit, I had a perfect view of her. Not someone I recognized. Good. If this mystery lady saw us, she wouldn't know who we were. Here they were, sitting so close to us. We didn't have to move. How cool was that? My heart thundered against my ribs. I caught my lower lip. Being a great detective involved some spying to collect information and I prayed for some good clues to lead us to the pineapple culprits — even if it included Brody.

My eyes darted from Maile to Sam. I placed a finger on my lips. They nodded.

"Thanks for coming." Brody's voice.

"I'll always come when you call." She gazed at him and leaned forward. Had she put a hand on his?

I couldn't see much anymore, and I didn't want to stretch upward. If she noticed, she might wonder if we were listening, maybe even want to move to another booth. That would ruin everything.

"Please tell me what happened today to make you so concerned."

Brody sighed. "It's Nico."

The guy we heard arguing with Brody and storming from his office.

Her voice turned quiet. "What about him?"

"He accused me of being behind the vandalism in the fields."

"Why would he think that?"

I shoved a fry in my mouth and waited for Brody's response.

"He thinks I'm trying to get a better position at one of the large plantations, and that I'm trying to make trouble for your family."

Did he say *your family*? I didn't understand. Did he mean the Tongs? If so, then who was Brody talking to? I scrunched my face. The only other Tong I knew about was Serena, but she was Nico's girlfriend. Why would Brody be meeting her?

"I can't believe he's accusing you."

The server placed three glasses of water on our table. I smiled. "Thanks."

She moved to Brody's booth. "What can I get you this afternoon?"

"Two coffees, please. And cream."

"Coming right up." The server left.

The woman made a little groaning noise. "I think I need to confront him."

"No, Serena."

I opened my eyes wide and stared at my two friends. What was going on?

"Brody, I need to do this before Nico goes any further. If my father hears about his accusations, he'll side with him."

The server brought their coffees, then left.

Brody took a noisy sip. "I don't want you to do anything. I'll find some way to handle Nico."

A spoon clinked in a mug — probably Serena stirring in cream. "What about the damage in the fields? If they catch the kids who are doing it, then Nico will back off."

"The police are driving by the fields occasionally, but they can't monitor all night."

"Maybe I can talk to my dad and get him to hire someone to watch the farm."

"No." A mug clunked on the table. "The plantation is suffering financially right now."

"But if he spent the money on security, it would eventually pay off. Otherwise, the vandalism might go on forever."

There was silence for a couple minutes. They must have been drinking coffee.

"Brody, I'm going to talk with my dad." She sighed. "But I promise not to confront Nico."

"Okay. And I'll see what I can do in the meantime." He paused. "But now I need to get back to work. There's a stack of paperwork waiting for me and it's not getting any smaller while I drink coffee with you."

"Aren't you off work?"

"Technically, but I have some things I want to get done before tomorrow."

Serena chuckled. "Always the dedicated employee."

They scooted out of the booth and sauntered to the front counter.

"Major cool." Sam leaned to the side and peered down the aisle.

I stretched up higher to see them over the top of the booths.

Maile scrunched her mouth to one side. "Yeah, but I don't understand any of it."

Brody paid the bill, then walked toward the door where Serena waited. He grabbed her shoulders and kissed her.

ʻUmikumamamakolu
(Thirteen)

"Whoa!" Sam plastered his back against the seat. "What was that all about?"

"What is it?" Maile rose up, turned and peeked over the booth, but, by that time, Brody and Serena had walked outside and were headed in opposite directions.

"I don't see anything. What happened, guys?" Maile's head moved back and forth as she scanned the area. "Uh-oh. I see Brody outside and he's coming this way." She turned and plopped down onto the seat.

I shielded my face and peered through my fingers at Brody trucking down the sidewalk past us. Once the danger of being discovered passed, I lowered my hand and shook my head.

"Is somebody going to tell me what happened?" Maile frowned and folded her arms across her chest. "I will never sit with my back to the action again."

I leaned on the table toward my friend. "They kissed."

"You're joking me, right?"

"Nope."

Sam jumped in. "I saw it too. Man! 'Bout died on the spot. I wanted to march up to that Brody guy and tell him off. What a creepo, huh? He's coming on to the boss' daughter. What's that all about, anyway? Maybe he really is trying to ruin the plantation."

"Man, Sam!" I snickered. "You sure can jump to conclusions. What makes you think Brody is guilty?"

He shrugged. "I don't know. He could be trying to frame Nico so he can have Serena."

"Yeah, well, it's a theory."

Maile waved her hands. "Hold on. It's way too early to make accusations. I think everybody's a suspect right now." She held up her fingers, one at a time. "There's Brody, Nico, Serena, Mr. Tong and even the mystery teens vandalizing for fun."

I nodded. "You're right."

Sam's face looked like a wrinkly prune. "I never thought about Serena. She could hate the plantation. Maybe she doesn't want to run the business, so she's trying to make it go away." He sat back. "The only thing is, don't know why she'd be hangin' with both Nico *and* Brody."

We sat in silence for a moment. Maile and Sam dipped fries. I drank some water. "I think the best way to find an answer is to stake out the plantation tonight."

Maile shook her head. "I don't think so. There's no way my mom is going to let me out of the house late at night, especially when we don't know how long it would take before someone came by."

Sam waved a fry in the air. "Yeah, and what if no one shows? We could be there forever."

"Okay, here's the plan." I wiped my face with a napkin. "We'll have to sneak out, 'cause none of our moms will let us go."

Maile cringed. "Oh, I don't know…"

"If you don't want to do it, I'll understand." I glanced at Sam.

"I think the whole thing is exciting. My mom would kill me if she found out, but I'm up for it."

Maile sighed. "I really don't want to miss out on this. Besides, what if we do discover the criminals? We'll be famous, and if my mom kills me, well, she'll be in deep trouble."

Our threesome burst out laughing. We were going to do it — a real stakeout — and probably catch a vandal.

Sam opened his mouth. "What time? When are all our parents asleep? That'd work. But where should we hook up and how long do we stay out?" Sam spilled a truckload of questions. "Do you think we should walk around the fields the whole time? Maybe just find a place to hide and wait for the jerko vandals? Don't know where those creepos have struck, but bet we'll smell the gross, moldy pineapples and probably see the nasty, squashed messes. Hope those weirdos haven't attacked everywhere, 'cause it'd be a lot easier if it was in one place."

"Wow! I think you've covered everything. Only, let's plan this one step at a time."

Maile nodded. "My mom and dad go to bed by 11 every night. My dad has to get up really early for work. I'm sure I could get out around midnight."

"Works for me too." I paused. "Sometimes Kimo stays up late playing video games, but I'll be really careful and completely quiet."

"No problem here. My parents are total 'early to bed' people." Sam grinned. "Now, where?"

"Let's meet at the main road straight across the fields from my house. It's not a far walk for any of us." I sipped some water. 'Course, that meant I'd have to walk through the same area where I had my stupid accident, but I'd be okay. "So, if we can all get out by midnight, let's meet at 12:30. And don't forget to bring a flashlight."

Maile combed a hand through her long hair. "What about finding the right spot to observe?"

"I still have Brody's number." I dug in my pack and pulled out my cell.

Maile smiled. "Hey. You remembered your phone."

"Yeah, well, Mom threatened to take it away if I kept leaving it at home."

"Bummer."

"I'll call Brody before he leaves work and ask him where the damage has been done. Then we should have an idea."

Sam slapped a hand on the table. "Great plan, Leilani. Can't wait for tonight."

Maile seemed worried. She put on a smile that looked a little forced. "I sure hope this whole thing pays off."

I glanced at my cell. "It will." I found Brody's number in my phone and selected it. Grinning at my friends, I waited as the phone rang in my ear.

Sam slammed his body close to mine and squeezed his ear against my phone to hear the conversation.

"Tong Plantation. Brody Trent speaking."

"Hi, Brody. This is Leilani Akamai. This morning you said I could call if we had anymore questions. I was wondering if I could ask you something."

"Sure."

"Do you know if the damage caused by the vandals has been in a certain area, or has it been all over the plantation?"

"Actually, it's been in a few random spots, but mostly not too far in from the main road that runs along the fields, closer to the beach side of the plantation. They've never struck near the buildings, probably because of the fear of being caught."

"Thank you so much."

"Wait. Why do you want to know?"

Nerves spiked through my body. "Just part of the project. We want to have all the facts and we forgot to ask you that question this morning. Thanks, bye." Hands shaking, I hung up before he could question me any further.

Maile squeezed her lips tight. "Again, I'm the one who's left out. What did he say?"

I smiled. "You'll get a front row seat tonight during our investigation. Promise." I motioned for Sam to scoot out of the booth. "Brody said it's been mostly close to the main road and near the beach side, far away from the Plantation offices and buildings." I grabbed the bill and stood. "Let's get going."

After paying, we made our way down the sidewalk to our bikes and helmets. We took off with Maile in the lead.

She yelled back at us. "I guess this is one thing I'm good at."

I laughed. "Yeah, you go, girl."

My two friends split off and headed to their houses while I continued to mine. My mind raced with possible scenarios. What was going on with Brody, Serena and Nico? Was Mr. Tong involved somehow? And our plan for tonight — how would it go? Would we catch someone in the act? Would we solve the case? A smile overtook my face. Everything was working out perfectly.

Then something wet hit my cheek — a drop of rain.

"Oh no! Not now." I pedaled faster, but the sky opened with a tropical downpour and I couldn't outrun the buckets of water spilling from above.

It soaked my cast.

Umikumamaha
(Fourteen)

"Oh, Leilani!" My mom stood in the kitchen with a pan of almond gelatin in her hand. "I can't believe you were out riding your bike in the pouring rain."

I stood there, water dripping off my helmet onto the floor. "It wasn't raining when I started. My legs just couldn't pedal fast enough to get home once it started." The Lord must have heard my comment about the area needing some rain, but did He have to send the downpour when I was out there with no protection for my arm?

Mom slipped the pan into the fridge and wiped her hands. "Let's go. You need to get a new cast."

"Great."

"Hey. I don't want to hear one complaint from you, missy. You're not the one who has to interrupt her day in order to correct the results of your bad judgment."

I sighed. "Sorry." Didn't it matter that *my* day was interrupted too? It wasn't like I planned to ruin my cast. "Guess I should have brought a bag or something just in case, huh?"

Mom nodded, then reached her arm out and pulled me close. "I know you weren't planning on being caught in the rain like that. I'm sorry I snapped at you." She squeezed. "I'm still trying to get used to not having your father around. It's hard when every little disaster falls on my shoulders."

"Did something else happen today?"

"Just a small plumbing problem. Nothing you need to worry about." She tweaked my nose. "Would you round up Kimo so we can get going?"

I nodded and trudged down the hall. My little brother was in his room, listening to iPod music through earphones and drawing in his art book.

"Hey, Kimo!"

He looked up and pulled off the headset. "What are you yelling about?"

"We need to go. Come on."

"Where? Mom said I could draw all afternoon."

I grabbed his arm and pulled him off the bed. "Well, things have changed." I glanced at the book and pencil, then reached for them. "You can bring these with you and work while we're at the clinic."

"The clinic? Is something wrong with Mom?"

"No. It's my cast. I got the stupid thing wet in the rain."

Groaning, Kimo stomped his way to the front of the house.

Mom was waiting there for us. "Okay, troops, let's head out."

The trip to the doctor gave me time to think about the midnight stakeout plan I had with Maile and Sam. I hoped Mom wouldn't find out. I'd hate to add even more to her stress. I prayed for God to give her strength to make it through each day without Dad.

We arrived at the clinic and marched through the front door. Maggie tapped on the computer at the front counter. Mom went through the insurance card ritual again and then we settled in to wait.

I figured the only good thing about this was that my mom would sleep well tonight. She seemed totally burned out. That meant my escape to the plantation would be easy, and I'd be undiscovered.

The magazines on the table hadn't changed—same old boring selection. I frowned and decided to watch people as they entered and left the building. What if one of them was the pineapple fields vandal? Right now I didn't have a clue. But after tonight...

I grinned at the thought of a successful stakeout, and prayed God would help us find and catch the criminal.

The squeaky front door distracted me. I stared at the two men entering. I didn't know the younger one, but the other one was Nico Hanes from earlier in the day. Slinking down in my chair, I hoped he wouldn't recognize me. When he stormed out of the plantation offices, his only mission seemed to be a quick exit, so I felt pretty sure he never noticed me.

He and the baldheaded man with a scruffy beard sat one seat away from me. I turned to somewhat hide my face, yet still see them and focus on their conversation.

Nico spoke first. "Thanks for meeting me here."

"No problem. I understand. But, the clinic?"

"Allergy shots. I get them on a regular basis so it's the perfect time and place."

"Good plan." The man nodded, light shining off his shaved scalp.

"This has to be kept between the two of us, okay?"

"Right."

What was the big secret? And why couldn't they meet at Nico's office? Brody said he was some kind of businessman, so wouldn't he have a private place?

Nico folded his hands and leaned forward, elbows resting on his knees. "Things aren't going well at the plantation right now, so it might be time to start planning."

Planning? For what?

"Sounds good to me. What do you want to do first?"

"Why don't you write up a proposal?"

My mind raced with a million questions. Did it have something to do with the damage in the fields? Maybe one of them would say what was going on.

"I can do that. How soon do you want it?"

"There's no rush." Nico rubbed his head. "It really depends on Serena."

Why would anything these two were discussing have something to do with Serena? 'Course, she was the owner's daughter. Maybe Maile was right. Could Serena or her dad have something to do with the vandalism of their own pineapple crops? But why would they do that? I saw in a movie once where a guy had financial problems and wanted to get insurance money or something, so he destroyed his business. Maybe that was it.

"How is your lovely lady these days?"

"Stubborn."

"Have you asked her to marry you?"

Oh no! What would happen if Nico asked Serena to marry him? What about Brody? I squirmed and rubbed my aching head.

"Not yet. Just like our deal, the timing for marriage has to be right."

I sighed. The whole conversation confused me.

"Leilani?" The nurse looked up from her clipboard. "We're ready for you."

I forced a smile and trudged toward her. No more conversation to hear, not that it made any sense.

The nurse led me to the cast room. "Sit up here and the technician will be with you shortly."

I yanked my phone from my pocket and called Maile at home since her mom still wouldn't replace her cell. I was surprised when she picked up the phone.

"Hey, Maile. Figured your mom would answer."

"When I got home, she and Kainoa were gone, so I'm alone. What's up?"

"My cast got wet in the rain today, so we're at the clinic getting a new one."

"Oh, man! I didn't even think about that when the rain started."

I spoke low and quiet. "Anyway, while I was in the waiting room, that Nico guy came in with some other man and they had a crazy conversation."

"What do you mean?"

"They were talking about some kind of proposal and keeping things quiet."

"That's kind of creepy."

"Yeah. They also talked about it being the right time with the plantation troubles and all. And the other man asked Nico if he was going to ask Serena to marry him."

"Wow!"

I spotted Dan-The-Cast-Man approaching. "Gotta go. Would you call Sam and fill him in?" I closed my phone. "Sorry. I'm not supposed to have this on in here, huh?"

He gave me a little stink-eye. "You must enjoy breaking rules. I'm surprised to see you back so soon. Not time to get rid of this thing yet." He lifted my cast. "What's up, anyway? You decide to take a dive in the ocean?"

I shook my head. "No. I got caught in a downpour." I narrowed my eyes. "And I'm not a rule-breaker. This wasn't my fault."

"Hmm. Not only a rule-breaker, but a feisty one." He winked. "Let's get you a new cast."

Dan worked fast, and before I could think too much about the weird conversation I'd overheard, I was on my way back to the lobby. He followed me and waved at my mom. "Make sure she keeps this one dry. It's not that I don't think she's adorable, but I really don't want her back again until the thing is ready to come off."

I turned and sneered at him.

My mom grinned and nodded. She ushered Kimo toward the door.

I stopped and motioned across the lobby. "Hey, Mom, I need to use the bathroom."

"Meet you at the car."

After leaving the restroom, I hustled toward the entry.

"Hey, Leilani! Wot's da haps?"

I looked toward the voice.

"Kainoa?"

ʻUmikūmāmālima
(Fifteen)

I stuttered. My mind went blank. Why was I here? Oh yeah …
"I — I got a new cast. Got the first one wet."

Kainoa chuckled. "Don't tell me you tried to surf in spite of
your arm."

I passed him a crooked smile. "Funny. The cast guy already
asked me pretty much the same thing."

"Knew you were in here since we ran into your mom and Kimo
in the parking lot. My mom is still outside talking to yours."

I focused on Kainoa and noticed he was holding a small cloth
in his hand. It appeared blood-streaked. "What did you do?"

"Nothing, really. Just trying to help Carly with her surfing."

Carly. The warm feeling inside froze and I gritted my teeth.

He turned and pointed to the side of his head. "Got whacked
by the crazy thing." He raised his hands. "Oh, but don't worry.
Your board is just fine."

I took a deep breath. Kainoa was okay and so was my board.
I caught his gaze with my eyes. "Too bad you got hurt. And I
know you're taking good care of my surfboard." I zoomed in on
his wet, matted hair. "Ouch. Looks painful."

"Mom freaked and figured I needed stitches. So, here I am."
He smiled.

A little heat bubbled inside. I had Kainoa to myself. No Carly around. "I guess I should let you get checked in."

He nodded. "No more water sports, Leilani." A sly grin slid across his lips.

"Hope you don't need stitches." I cocked my head. "But, I do have a warning for you."

"Yeah?"

"Beware of your chart. It might tell your doctor you need a tetanus shot."

He cringed.

I smiled at his contorted face, turned and marched out the door.

Mrs. O lumbered through the parking lot. We waved and I stepped up my pace. I figured Mom would be anxious to get home and start dinner, and I should probably help her out. I didn't want to be on her bad side. If she were to somehow find out about my late-night adventure with Maile and Sam, it would help my case if she weren't already annoyed with me.

*****

Once home, I headed to my room and grabbed my iPod. I placed the headphones over my ears and quick-stepped to the kitchen.

Mom paraded in at about the same time, opened the fridge and pulled out a package of shrimp.

"Need some help with dinner, Mom?" I removed one of the earpieces.

She stared at me, eyes narrowed. "It's very nice of you to offer, but I think I have it under control."

"You sure?"

She placed the wok on the stove and smiled. "Maybe you're right. I'm making a shrimp stir-fry. There are lots of vegetables to cut up. If you can manage with your right hand cutting and your left fingers holding, do you want to start on those?"

"Sure."

"Here." She snatched a plastic glove from a drawer. "Put this on your left hand to protect the lower part of your cast."

"Thanks." For sure, I didn't want to soak the thing with veggie juice. I grabbed the cutting board, then made my way to the refrigerator bin. "Broccoli, peppers, green onions, zucchini and carrots. Anything else?"

"Yeah. Take out some tomatoes. We'll have those in chunks on top."

I plopped the bags on the counter near the cutting board, then replaced my earpiece. Chopping and swaying to the music in my ears, I kept my fingers out of the way. I may not be a klutz when it came to athletics, but food preparation was a whole new world for me. Maybe since I was now 13, I should learn how to cook. Mom was a great cook. Dad always complimented and thanked her for every dinner. I was sure she missed that. Especially when Kimo whined about things he didn't like. 'Course, I was guilty too. I chopped some more.

Mom touched my back and peeked over my shoulder.

I pulled the earpieces out, letting them dangle around my neck.

"Looks good, sweetie."

"This is kinda fun. Maybe I'll help more often."

She grinned. "I'm not going to hold my breath, but I'm appreciating the moment."

I finished up the last few green onion stalks, carried the full board to the wok and plopped the veggies in.

"You and your friends have any plans for tomorrow?"

I shrugged. She didn't ask about tonight. Or — was after midnight really tomorrow? Oh, man! I hated to lie.

"Not really. I think we'll talk later and make some plans."

"All I ask is, protect that cast, okay?"

Nodding, I prepared to slice the tomatoes, but stopped. "Maybe I shouldn't do this part. These things are so juicy and messy. I might ruin my cast again, even with the glove on."

"Good point." She grabbed the knife. "Why don't you start the burner and I'll slice."

"You got it." I replaced the ear-buds, danced over to the stove and turned up the gas. Wooden spoon in hand, I watched the olive oil sizzle and stirred the veggies. A great song blasted in my ears. Waving the utensil around, I hopped in a circle. I loved to dance. Thank goodness it was one thing I could still do with a broken arm.

Eyes closed, my head bopped to the rhythm. I could feel the bass guitar pounding in my head, but the drums were the best. They really inspired me to get down and crazy. The beat seemed to vibrate in my chest. Sliding from side to side, I whipped my ponytail back and forth. I was a great dancer.

Suddenly, the sound wasn't right. I opened my eyes and saw Mom waving the knife and heading toward me. Realizing she was yelling, I whipped around and saw the smoking black mass in the bottom of the wok.

Umikumamaono
(Sixteen)

I turned off the gas, yanked the pan from the burner and pulled the music from my ears.

Fanning the air with a dishtowel, Mom flew across the kitchen. "Leilani! What were you doing dancing all around like that? You were supposed to be watching the vegetables."

The room smelled super gross. A smoky, gray haze hung above us, not unlike the cloud inside me. "Mom, I'm so sorry. The dinner is totally ruined."

She flicked the stove fan on high and waved the cloth some more. Some of the smog snaked upward into the vent. I plopped onto a kitchen chair and hung my head. Now I realized how Kimo felt the day he exploded the guava cake. "I guess you've been cursed with two kids who can't cook." I scanned the scene. "I shouldn't be allowed to step into a kitchen."

Mom peered at the scorched mess. "I think all of the vegetables need a quick burial, but at least the shrimp and sauce weren't in there." She dumped the charred gunk into the trashcan, then set the blackened pan in the sink and filled it with water.

She turned, walked toward me and slipped an arm around my shoulder. "No problem, sweetie. You should have seen me the first time I tried to cook. Your disaster is nothing like what mine was. So, you see, you and Kimo inherited my wonderful culinary abilities."

"Really?"

"Yup." She flicked my ponytail, then squeezed me tight. "Now let's get the rest of the veggies and start this whole thing over again."

Kimo scurried into the kitchen. He stopped short and looked up at the hovering smog. "Whoa! What happened?"

"Just a small kitchen accident." Mom placed her hands on his shoulders and ushered him out. "You go read or something. We'll call you when dinner's ready."

"Did Leilani do this? Ha! Ha! She can't cook either. At least I didn't almost burn the house down." His words faded as he skipped down the hall.

I sighed. My little twit of a brother was right. I sure hoped the investigation in the middle of the night would go better than the whole dinner thing.

After we devoured the second-chance meal, I volunteered to load the dishwasher while Kimo hunkered down with his favorite video game. Clean-up was a lot easier and less dangerous than cooking.

Mom sighed. "I'm really tired. Think I'll call it a night."

I hugged her, then dashed down the hall to my room and hopped onto the bed. A gentle wind blew through my window, causing the curtains to flutter. My nostrils filled with sweet scent. I loved the flowery smell of an island breeze.

Anxious for the midnight stakeout, I put together a little emergency kit. My mini-backpack worked well. I refilled my water bottle and stuffed it in. Some bandages, tissues, house key and a flashlight completed the special bag.

Snatching my favorite mystery book, I wondered how I

could possibly concentrate on reading when a super-secret mission in the pineapple fields lay ahead. Were Maile and Sam excited too?

I grabbed my phone and set the alarm for midnight. A shiver zipped through my back. My track record lately didn't make me confident everything would go smoothly tonight, let alone perfect.

Book in hand, I snuggled into the pillows and read.

*****

The annoying chiming of my cell phone woke me.

Little lightning bolts of excitement shot through my body. I stood and slipped into a light sweater. Before pocketing my cell, I silenced it. All I needed was a noisy phone waking up my mom or Kimo.

I peeked out my bedroom door and scanned the area. Silence. It seemed everyone was asleep, but I decided not to leave through the front entry. Floorboards creaking, or the front door squeaking, could wake them. Out the window was a better choice.

Although it was slightly open, there wasn't enough room to allow me to escape. I grasped it, pushed and cringed as the old thing groaned when I inched it upward. Stopping for a moment, I listened for any sounds of Mom or Kimo. Nothing. After lifting the window far enough to allow my body to squeeze through, I ducked under and out. Swinging one leg outside, I struggled to adjust my body without making any noise. Finally, the other leg. Yes! I'd made it.

Now, all I had to do was jump. I was on the ground level, but the house sat on a slight hill. Well, that was the first thing I hadn't thought about. I hoped there would be nothing else

I'd forgotten. Scooting my rear end as far forward as possible, I prayed I would make it to the ground without hurting myself.

I drew in a big breath, pushed my feet against the house and leaned forward. Remembering to bend my knees, I hit the ground with a thud, toppled over and groaned as the flashlight, water bottle and some branches poked my back. Lying quiet, I listened. Had Mom or Kimo heard my crash landing?

No sounds came from the house, and no lights flicked on. I stood and adjusted the backpack. Each careful, quiet step brought me closer to the plantation. Although the moonlight reflecting off the distant water beyond somewhat brightened the area, I still needed the flashlight.

I reached the fields and my trek between rows of pineapples began. I grimaced while moving through the rows where I'd crashed and burned. The pain still hung in my memory. Further along, I noticed a bunch of crushed fruit. It seemed to be one of the vandalized areas. A shiver ran along my spine and tingled through my arms. The weird combination of fear and excitement sent my feet pounding harder and faster. Thoughts of catching a criminal in the act paraded through my head.

As soon as I'd made it to the other side, next to the road, I glanced around, but saw no one. Silence was kind of a scary thing. Humming to myself, I continued to survey the area. Where were Sam and Maile?

Two small specks of light caught my attention. They were coming from up the road. I grinned and turned off my flashlight. My friends were coming. Now all we needed were the culprits to show up. I started to walk toward the moving specks.

The lights grew closer and I heard talking…a girl, but I didn't recognize the voice as Maile's. I couldn't make out any words, but definitely not my friends talking. Guys voices too.

I squatted and took shelter behind a pineapple plant. Had they seen me? My hands shook and the back of my neck tingled. At least I'd turned off my flashlight. And theirs were pointed at the road, not toward me. Still, my stomach sloshed like a washing machine.

Peeking between spiky leaves, I saw the lights turn away from the road and into the fields. They weren't close, but in the quiet of the night, I made out most of their conversation. Did they even care someone might hear them? Guess not. We were fairly far from any houses.

The first voice I heard was male. "This is going to be fun."

He didn't sound like an adult. Could the police be right? Was it just teenagers looking for thrills?

Then, a second male. "Yeah. What a blast! And to think your uncle is paying us for all this fun."

Someone was paying them? Man, these guys were cocky.

The third voice was female. "Typical guys. You only think about having fun."

"Hey, I figure if you can't get a little enjoyment out of life, you might as well pack it in. Besides, I know you like to have a good time. That's why I invited you."

Anger simmered inside me. What total jerks. I wanted to jump up and run toward them, screaming at the top of my lungs.

"Okay, so you got me." She giggled. " 'Course, the danger is kind of exciting too."

I gulped. That voice. I knew it.

Carly Rivers.

Umikumamahiku

(Seventeen)

Even though Carly was a self-centered snob, I never thought she'd be involved in something criminal. Why would she do this? And who were her friends? The police got it kind of right. Teens were involved, but paid by someone else.

The three jerks yelled and laughed. They stomped, and I cringed. I pictured beautiful pineapples crushed and ground into the dirt.

Peeking through plants, I saw the group moving around, their lights flickering back and forth. Time to make my move. I hunched and scooted onto the road. Prickly leaves jabbed me as I moved along the edge of the fields like a snake, one row… two…three. I slipped between plants and hunkered down. The vandals were only a couple rows away.

Where were Sam and Maile? I needed their help and advice. Had they fallen asleep and weren't coming? If they were just late, they'd walk into this disaster.

The threesome continued to laugh, cut plants and smash fruit. Maybe if I yelled really loud, it might scare them off. If I put on my biggest, deepest voice, hollered as loud as I could and waved the flashlight around, maybe they'd think I was the police or something.

But what if they didn't? I gulped. What made me think I could ever be a real detective? I didn't know what to do, and everything loomed huge and scary before me like one of Kimo's monster movies. But the longer I sat there, smelling the sweet scent of crushed pineapples, the more violent the frustration boiled inside.

Wild laughter and whooping reached my ears.

I stood. Flashlight in hand, I clicked it on and waved it at the three vandals. I stomped onto the road, and yelled loud and deep. "What's going on? What are you doing in these fields?"

They froze.

My mouth dried up and my tongue felt too big to stay inside.

One of the males took a step toward the road. "Who are you? You're definitely no cop."

My flashlight wavered all over as my hand shook uncontrollably. "The police are coming."

He belly-laughed. "Yeah, right."

I gripped the light tighter and tried to control its wavering. Maybe I could aim it into the guy's eyes. Praying the nausea would go away and my body would stop shaking, I swallowed hard and shined the beam on his face.

"Hey!" He shielded his eyes, but not before I got a decent look at him.

"You're in major trouble."

The second teen moved toward his buddy. Again, I aimed the light. He cringed, blinked and turned a bit. "You're the one who's in trouble, you little punk."

I didn't get a great look at his face. From the corner of my eye, I could see the first guy move closer to the road. I whipped the beam toward him. It glinted off something in his hand — a knife.

I hadn't thought about that before I confronted them. Of course they had a knife. How else would they cut off the pineapples?

Gulping, I tried to rid my throat of whatever seemed to be blocking my voice. My legs morphed into soggy noodles. Would I faint? Suddenly, energy appeared from nowhere and shot through my body. "Stop right there!"

He waved the knife around. "What ya gonna do? Come closer and you can meet my little friend, Mr. Blade."

Yeah, what was I going to do? I could run…or collapse and play dead. Maybe then they'd just leave, and I could die for real and melt into the ground.

The one with the knife moved toward me.

Dear Lord, please help me. What I needed was an officer to somehow appear. My heart thumped against my ribs and a shudder snaked its way up my spine. Then I heard Carly's voice.

"Hey, you guys! She's a girl."

Had she recognized me?

She stomped toward the guy still in the fields and grabbed his arm. "Come on, let's get out of here."

Yes, please just leave.

The knife-holder bellowed. "No way! This chick's got to pay for causing us trouble."

Carly shoved the other guy to the side and marched up to the knife-holder. She grabbed his arm. "Let's go." Her tone was deep and firm, unlike her usual nauseating high-pitched voice.

I stepped backward. Would they chase me if I turned and ran? What if they caught me? I wiped a sleeve across my sweaty forehead.

He focused past Carly and glared at me. His knife slashed

through the air. "You ready for some of this?"

Frozen, I almost threw up, but managed to whip out a few loud words. "Stay away from me!" I swallowed hard to keep my raging stomach contents in place.

Lights appeared in the distance behind him. I blinked and tilted my head to see them better. They bobbed up and down and grew larger as they closed in. Shouts hit my ears.

"What are you doing? Leave her alone and get out of here!" Maile's voice.

I sighed and willed my rubbery legs to step forward.

"The police are coming, you jerks." Sam's voice roared deep and loud. "You're going to be arrested, creepos."

Carly yelped and shoved the guy with the knife. "Out of my way!"

Everything happened at once. Carly and the other guy ran down the road, nearly plowing over my two friends. Shouts and shrieks flew from their mouths as Maile and Sam bombarded the knife guy. A blur of arms, flashlights and gleaming blade raged before me. My body quivered.

"Stop! You might get hurt."

They probably couldn't hear me over their bellowing. Sam's voice vibrated in my ears. "Think you're a big scary man with a knife, huh?" A thwack sounded as Sam landed his flashlight into the side of the guy's head.

Fear for my friends steaming in my stomach like a volcanic, sulfur lake, I bulleted forward, keeping my light on the blade. The guy held his arm across his face in an obvious attempt to protect it from the pelting flashlights. If it wasn't so scary, I might have laughed at Maile and Sam. They were beating him pretty well with those pretend weapons.

The guy raised his knife blade as if ready to attack. Shrieking,

I charged forward. I set my jaw and whacked his hand hard with my cast. The knife flew into darkness.

He grabbed his wrist. "You little jerk!" A string of not-so-nice-words spilled from his mouth.

"Kinda hurt, huh?" I squeezed my mouth tight and blasted a huge dose of evil-eye at him.

"You're going to pay." Jogging down the road after his buddy and Carly, he shouted over his shoulder. "You and your friends had better watch your backs."

I shuddered. What kind of mess did I just get us all into?

"Man, that was super scary." Maile reached for me. "You okay, Leilani? That guy was a major creep."

"I'll be better once my heart stops beating up my ribs."

Sam waved his almost-a-weapon around. "That weirdo had a knife. Glad we had these flashlights. Did we look crazy or what? I clobbered his head real good a couple times. Hope he has a huge headache. And, wow! Leilani, you were so cool when you smacked that knife right out of his hand. Kinda gutsy."

Maile sighed and wrinkled her nose. "Sorry we took so long to get here, but Sam's parents decided, for some strange reason, to stay up late and watch a movie. He tried to call you, but you must have turned off your phone. Then I called him 'cause I was having the same problem with my parents." She gulped. "So we couldn't do anything but wait."

I shrugged. "It's okay, but I sure am glad you showed up when you did."

"Were you scared?"

"Duh! Terrified is a much better word." My whole body continued to shake.

Maile narrowed her eyes. "Was that Carly?"

"Yup."

Sam shook his head. "Man, that girl is a real piece of work."

I gloated inside, but hoped it didn't shine through to the outside. "I have some things to tell you two, but we'd better meet tomorrow. It's too creepy out here right now."

Maile nodded. "I agree. Be careful walking back."

I waved at my friends and hustled through the fields toward home. The entire stakeout scene played in my mind. The visions spurred me to move faster. I was never so happy to see my house.

Glad I'd remembered to bring a key, I tiptoed up the stairs and unlocked the front door. I opened it a slit and peeked inside. Everything was dark except the kitchen stove light and a small entry lamp. No sounds, so I pushed the door further and slipped in. I shuffled across the floor and down the hall to my room. My sweaty hands shook as I opened my bedroom door. I'd made it. A successful stakeout with lots of new clues.

But before I could move inside, I heard a creak. I turned toward the noise.

Kimo.

Umikumamawalu
(Eighteen)

He was outside his room, standing in the hall. His arms were folded across his chest and a huge smirk consumed his face. "I saw you."

I put on my best innocent look. "Saw me what? Go to the kitchen to get a glass of water?"

"Oh yeah? With your backpack?"

"What do you care if I take my bag with me?"

Kimo danced down the hall toward me. "You didn't go to the kitchen. I saw you jump down from your window."

"What? Are you insane or something? You must have been dreaming."

"Nope. I was playing video games without the sound, 'cause Mom would get mad if she caught me up so late."

"Yeah, well she's going to be mad you're up now, bothering me."

He moved close and twisted his lips. "I heard a noise outside, so I looked and saw you climbing from your window. And then you jumped. I wanted to laugh and laugh. You looked so dorky when you smashed down onto your behind." He cocked his head. "Did you go someplace to get clues about the mystery?"

It seemed Kimo was not going to give up. I set my jaw and spoke quiet, yet firm words. "You're crazy. Good-night."

"No! I'm going to tell Mom unless you let me help you with the Detective Club stuff."

"What?"

"I want to help. I know lots of stuff."

"Yeah, yeah. You've said that before. And I told you if something came up where we could use you, I'd let you know."

"Well, I don't believe you." He stuck his tongue out at me. "So now you *have* to let me help."

I sighed. "Okay, fine, you little twerp. I'll talk to you tomorrow."

"Yay, yay, yay!" Kimo popped up and down like a little bouncy ball. Wasn't he tired at all?

"Shhhh!" I waved my hand at him. "You're going to wake Mom."

"Sorry." He slapped both hands over his mouth and shuffled down the hall. Before entering his room, he turned and pantomimed an *okay sign*, a zip across his lips, and then a wild wave and airborne kisses.

Stifling a giggle, I shook my head and slipped into my room. Great. Now I'd have to let Kimo tag along with me. How would I explain that to Maile and Sam?

I sighed and tossed my pack on the floor. Every move seemed sluggish as I changed and climbed into bed. I groaned, rolled over and snuggled into the pillow. I'd worry about Kimo tomorrow.

*****

A loud noise startled me. Squinting against the streaming sunlight invading my room, I focused on the sound. Pounding. Then I heard yelling.

"Wake up, Leilani!"

"Go away, Kimo." Why was he waking me up so early? He

should be tired since he was up half the night too. I pulled a pillow over my ear with one hand and grabbed some covers with the other. The annoying voice and pounding still echoed.

"Mom says breakfast is ready. You'd better get up or she'll wonder –"

"Okay! I'm up." I rolled over and stuck my legs out from under the sheet. "Just stop that pounding and yelling, okay?"

"Can I come in?"

Kimo did *not* need to come into my room. I started to answer with a big *no*, but decided it wouldn't be very smart. "I guess."

The door creaked open and Kimo stuck his head through the gap. "Hurry and eat so we can plan after that."

"What?"

"You know." A smile spread across his face. "The plan for how I'm going to help you and Maile and Sam."

Oh, man, I still hoped maybe last night had been a bad dream. No such luck. How would I ever get out of this mess? Best plan of attack — play along. "Yeah. We'll talk after breakfast."

"Cool, cool, cool!" He shut the door, but I could still hear his little sing-song voice floating down the hall. "I'm going to be a real detective and solve the case. Yes!"

Pictures of me dragging Kimo along today played out in my mind. Kimo gloating, me frowning, and Maile and Sam staring with open mouths. I grimaced. Yeah, this was going to be a great day.

I shuffled to the bathroom, the lack of sleep making me feel like a zombie. Maybe after I ate something, my energy level would improve. I splashed water on my face and pulled my hair into a ponytail. The reflection in the mirror told me I looked almost human.

I dragged myself to the table and plopped into a chair. The aroma of eggs and bacon filled my nostrils. "Mmm. Smells great, Mom."

"You're normally up earlier than this, sweetie. You feeling okay?" She set a full plate in front of me.

Yup, I was used to getting up super early to catch those first waves of the day. Sure missed my surfing routine. I shrugged. "Yeah, just a little tired." I glanced at Kimo.

He squirmed in his chair and made a silly face.

I shot him a heap of mean-mouth.

Mom cracked open an egg and it splatted onto the grill. "What are you doing today, meeting up with your friends?"

I picked up a piece of bacon. "Yup."

Kimo sat up tall in his seat. "And Leilani said I can go with her."

I nearly choked on my food.

"Oh, is that so?" She flipped an egg.

Kimo nodded like a yo-yo.

I glared at him.

"Have you forgotten something?" Mom turned and raised her brow at him.

"No, I don't think so."

Mom shoveled up a couple eggs, trucked them over to the table and slid them onto Kimo's plate. "Kimo?"

"What? I can't go with Leilani?"

She cocked her head and placed a hand on her hip.

"Mahhhhhm! Why can't I?"

The conversation was getting really interesting. Was Mom going to save my day? I couldn't figure out why she wasn't going to let Kimo go with me, but it didn't matter. The thought of my little brother having to stay home and do whatever it was Mom needed him to do sent a bolt of energy through my body. Suddenly, I was ready to face the day.

Mom headed back to the stove and pulled bacon from the pan and onto a plate. "Don't you remember what I told you this year during school?"

Kimo shrugged. "You always yelled at me about doing my homework instead of drawing."

"Yes. And?"

"I don't know."

"Kimo, I know you love your art, and I love how talented you are, but I told you if you didn't start working harder, I'd have to do something about it." She stared at him.

He groaned and stabbed an egg with his fork. "But if I didn't do good in math, does that mean you're gonna make me stay home and do math stuff with you?"

She sighed, cocked her head and stared at him. "I signed you up."

"For what?"

"Summer school. You start today."

Umikumamaiwa
(Nineteen)

"No fair, Mom!"

I tried not to grin. "Man, Kimo, what a bummer. Summer school."

He slammed back into his chair and folded both arms across his chest. "Yeah, Leilani, like you really care."

Kimo was right, but he was wrong too. I was glad he wouldn't be tagging along, but I felt sorry for him at the same time. He really wanted to be part of the investigation and help me. What could I do to make him feel involved?

Wiping my mouth, I stood, then tossed the napkin on the table and moved behind Kimo's chair. I whispered in his ear. "Hey, kiddo. When you're done with school, Maile, Sam and I will come back here and fill you in on stuff. Then you can help us plan the next step, okay?"

He nodded without smiling.

Every memory I had of Kimo included a smiling face and a bopping body. Seeing him slumped in a chair wearing a scowl kind of bothered me. My heart panged a little. Where was the Kimo I knew and loved? Yes, I really did love my annoying, idiotic, crazy little brother. I sighed and squeezed his shoulders. "Do well in school and I'll see you later."

I paused a moment and stared at the back of his head. Slouched in his chair, Kimo didn't say a word.

"Mom, I'm going to meet up with Maile and Sam."

"Okay. When do you plan to be home?"

"This afternoon. Maybe around two or so."

"If I'm not home, I'll be picking up Kimo from school and getting some groceries. I figured you two would appreciate having some dinner tonight — other than toast and peanut butter, that is. 'Course, I could always get you to cook." She chuckled and winked at me.

"Funny, Mom." I took one last look at my scowling brother and shuffled off to call my friends. We had so much to do and talk about before we could solve the mystery. I grabbed my cell and called Maile's house.

She whispered. "Hey, Leilani. You got home okay last night?"

"Yeah, no accidents. I still have one good arm and two good legs."

She giggled. "Where do you want to meet this morning?"

"I was hoping your house."

"Okay."

"Does Kainoa have a yearbook from high school?"

"Yeah."

"Do you think you can get hold of it? Maybe we can find a picture of the guys from last night."

"I can try. Kainoa's surfing right now."

"Great. I'll call Sam and be over in a bit."

Sam was calm about things, as usual. "What a night, huh? Couldn't sleep much, kept rolling around in my bed and thinking about stuff. That knife guy was insane, and crazy Carly's involved with the creep." He crunched some kind of food in my ear.

I strained to catch his munching words.

"She's hooked up with some real bad dudes, huh? Well, see you at Maile's. Bye."

The phone clicked in my ear. I didn't even get to tell him anything about digging through the yearbook. Didn't matter, I'd talk with both my friends soon.

A knock on my door startled me. "Yeah?"

"Sweetie, I'm leaving to take Kimo to school. You want a ride to Maile's or Sam's?"

"Thanks, Mom. That'd be cool. I'll be right out."

Grabbing my things, I mentally ran through the events of last night. It seemed, the more I discovered, the more questions it created.

I made my way out of the house and joined Mom and Kimo in the car. Glancing at my brother in the back seat, I noted the frown highlighting his face. "Hey, kiddo, you're going to do a great job with your math class. You can tell me all about it later today, okay?"

He twisted his mouth and nodded.

I grinned and shot a thumbs-up his direction.

During the ride, I made a mental list of questions to answer and things to do.

First, tell my friends about the conversation between Nico and the unknown man at the clinic. Second, try to figure out who the two guys were at the pineapple fields last night. Third, why and how was Carly involved in this mess? Fourth, since Carly was involved, was Kainoa too?

I gulped hard. That thought hadn't come into my mind before, but now…could Kainoa be involved?

Fifth, what was up with Brody and Serena? Sixth, I wanted to confront Carly about what she and her two friends had done. Number six was pretty ugly. I shuddered at the thought of what she might do if she found out it was me, Maile and Sam in the pineapple fields last night.

We pulled up to Maile's house.

"See you later, sweetie. Have fun." Mom turned and leveled her eyes with mine. "And protect that cast. I do *not* want to have to make another trip to the doctor." Her brow puckered as she glanced at my arm. "That thing looks pretty dirty and battered. What have you been doing, mud wrestling?"

I smiled, but cringed on the inside. Glancing at Kimo, I saw a grin spread across his face. I held a finger to my lips.

After jumping from the truck's running board, I jogged down the path to the Onakeas' front steps. Before I made it up the steps to the lanai, though, Maile bounded out the door. "Hey, got Kainoa's yearbook."

"Cool. Sam here yet?"

"Yeah. He said you didn't tell him about the whole yearbook thing."

"Well, duh! Have you ever tried to get a sound in, let alone an entire thought, when his words are charging you like a bull?"

Maile burst out laughing just as Sam walked up behind her.

"Glad I can make you guys laugh." Arms folded across his chest, he shot a fiery stare at me.

"Sorry, Sam." I cocked my head and tried to put on my best sad-puppy-dog eyes. "You know we love you."

"Ditto." Maile turned, grabbed Sam and reached for me. "Group hug!"

Maile and I giggled and squeezed. Sam kept his arms to his sides and grunted, but seemed to tolerate us. "Girls and hugging — gross."

I really hoped Mrs. O wasn't around the corner watching, worse, yet, Kainoa.

Maile pulled me inside. "Come on, let's get to some major sleuthing."

On the way to Maile's room, I noticed her mom working in the kitchen. I stopped. "Hi, Mrs. O."

"Hello there, Leilani." She wiped her hands on a towel. "How's that arm of yours doing?"

"Good." I held up the cast.

"And how long do you have to be imprisoned in that thing?"

I shrugged. "Most of the summer, I guess."

She moved close and touched my shoulder. "It's rough, huh, missing the whole summer surfing season?"

"Yeah, but I'm okay."

"You three kids have fun today. Doing anything special?"

I shook my head. "Just hanging out."

"Let's go, Leilani." Maile's voice floated from the hallway. My two friends approached.

"Bye, Mom. We're going to hit the beach for a while." Grinning, Maile flashed the yearbook in front of me.

We made our way through the house and plodded toward the sand. The sun flickered through palm fronds and reflected off the water like little sparklers on the fourth of July. The sounds of waves rolling in and crashing onto shore vibrated in my ears. Eyes closed, I inhaled the salty air.

Sam jogged toward our spot — the place where, for several years, we had held regular meetings of The Hawaiian Island Detective Club. We'd had a blast. Would trying to solve a real crime be as much fun? So far, it had just been frustrating...and creepy.

Maile and I reached the palms right behind Sam. He plopped onto the sandy soil. "Okay, let's see that book."

We sat, Maile in the middle.

"I saw one of the guys pretty clearly." I leaned over the book. "I'll recognize him, and maybe the other guy too."

Sam frowned. "How come you think their pictures are in here?"

I shrugged. "Don't, but they knew Carly, so I'm hoping they go to school with her and Kainoa."

"Great detective work." Maile turned pages. "So let's start with the sophomore class."

I focused on each picture. "Nope."

Again and again I shook my head as Maile turned pages. Nothing.

"That's it for the sophomores." Maile flipped a page. "Want to try the juniors?"

"Yeah. They could be older." Again, she turned pages and I shook my head.

Then I saw him — the knife-wielding creep. I shuddered and pointed a shaky finger. "There's one of them." I leaned in close and read the name. "George Hanes."

Maile frowned. "Hanes? Where have I heard that name before?"

Iwakalua
(Twenty)

It came to me. "At the plantation…Nico Hanes."

Sam tipped his head. "Isn't he Serena Tong's boyfriend? Or is she actually Brody's girlfriend?" He grimaced. "All this love stuff is way stupid." Sam fixed his gaze on the photo. "Think this George guy is related to Nico?"

I held up my hand. "Whoa, Sam. Let me tell you what I overheard last night." I leaned in closer to my friends. Didn't know why, only the palm trees and distant surfers might hear. But since we were real detectives, it made everything super secretive.

"Before you guys showed up last night, those two creeps and Carly came down the road."

"Don't you mean *three* creeps?" Maile snickered. "Sorry. Wasn't nice, huh?"

I squeezed my lips together to stop a grin from popping out. Maile had said exactly what I'd thought. "Anyway, I ducked behind some pineapple plants and listened. One of the guys said something about how nice it was that the other's uncle paid them to trash the fields."

Sam's brows lifted high above his eyes. "So you're thinkin' maybe Nico is George's uncle?"

I nodded. "Could be."

Maile looked up. "So, what do we do now?"

"Keep looking for the other guy." I pointed at the book.

Maile flipped through a chunk of pages. "Let's look at the other classes and see if maybe he's older or younger than this George guy."

We searched every page. Nothing.

Maile closed the yearbook, planted an elbow on its cover and rested her chin on one hand.

Sam had a thought. "The other guy must go to a private school, or could be older and already graduated. Doesn't matter 'cause we have one of them nailed, and maybe even have a connection to that strange man, Nico." He frowned. "I thought he was totally weird."

I nodded. "Yeah."

"He was more than that." Maile lifted her chin. "He creeped me out."

"Did you tell Sam about the other day in the clinic?"

"What?" Sam narrowed his eyes and glued his stare on me as if I was about to reveal something top secret.

"Yesterday, when I was getting a new cast —"

Sam jerked. "Another one? What happened? You break something else?"

I shook my head. "No. Everything's been so crazy lately that I forgot to tell you about my bike ride home from The Coffee House. Everything was cool, and I rode just fine, but then the rain came and ruined my cast."

Laughing, Sam shook his head. "Sorry. I didn't think about that. Bet your mom freaked, huh? I know if I had a cast and ruined it, my mom would go ballistic. She'd ground me from chips, cookies, ice-cream and all my video games for a year."

"Yeah. She wasn't happy, for sure." I drew in a breath. "The weird thing is, while I was at the clinic, Nico Hanes came in and met with another guy."

"Huh?"

I filled Sam in about the strange conversation. "Sorry I didn't keep you in the loop about this."

Maile nudged him. "I totally forgot to tell you."

"No pro-blem-o. We were kinda pumped about the stake-out. But I only forgive one time, so you'd better not leave me hangin' again or you'll be sorry." Sam wagged a finger back and forth. "Remember, I'm pretty good with a flashlight." He belly-laughed.

I raised my hands in surrender. "Funny, Sam. Don't worry, next time I won't depend on Maile's Message Service."

"Yeah, right." Maile sneered and swatted me. "You'll always depend on me."

Nodding, I smiled. "Yup. What would I do without the two of you?"

Maile laughed and raised her hands. "Hawaiian Island Detective Club forever!"

The three of us high-fived.

I shook my head. "I hope no one can see us. They'd know for sure we're a bunch of nerds."

"Maile's got it right." Sam shrugged. "The club isn't the same. It's morphed into something bigger and way cool. We're real detectives now, and once we solve this crime –"

"We're not going to solve anything unless we figure out the next step." I pulled out my notebook and pen. "I'm going to make a list of the people we need to interview."

"Brody and Nico, for sure." Maile sighed. "I hate to say it, but I think we need to talk to Carly too."

I scribbled the names. "Yup. Definitely."

"Leilani?"

"Yeah?" I looked up from my notebook and stared at Maile. Her brow pulled tight between her eyes and the normal glint in her pupils fogged over. "Is something wrong?"

"I just realized. If Carly is involved in the vandalism, then maybe Kainoa is too."

"Same thing's been bothering me, but I can't imagine your brother being part of it. He's too into his Hawaiian heritage and island culture." I touched Maile's hand. "Don't worry, I'm sure he's not involved."

Sam shook his head. "If Carly's involved, Kainoa would totally hate it." He shrugged. "Even though she looks like some supermodel, he'd for sure stop with the whole infatuation-with-Carly-Rivers thing."

I knew Sam was a typical guy and he was only trying to help, but did he have to compare her to a supermodel? As if I didn't already know I was a little nothing compared to her? But Kainoa may not believe it and would just defend her. I sighed. "Yeah, let's hope Kainoa will see through that prissy snob."

Maile leaned over and looked at my notes. "So, who do you want to talk to first?"

"Let's head over to the plantation offices. Maybe Brody can answer some questions."

"Good idea, but it's kind of far from here."

I shoved the pad into my backpack. "I have an idea, but first I've got to tell you guys something you're not going to like."

"What?" Maile puckered her lips into a little pout. "What else could possibly have gone wrong?"

"Kimo caught me last night."

"Oh, man, Leilani. How did that happen?"

"He was awake and heard me climbing out the window. He waited for me to come home and then confronted me."

Sam narrowed his eyes. "I don't understand. If he told your mom, you wouldn't be here today, right?"

"He only threatened to tell her. Basically, he blackmailed me."

Maile winced. "What do you have to do to keep your brother quiet?"

I tensed. "Let him help us."

"You're messing with us, right?"

Squeezing my lips tight, I shook my head.

"So where is the little blackmailer?" Maile peeked around a palm trunk. "Spying on us?"

"Nope. He's in summer school."

"Great!" Sam sighed. "I mean, I like Kimo. We're pretty good buds, but sometimes he drives me a little crazy. We just need to get out of here and go do our investigation before he's done with school."

"Yeah, but I promised him I'd let him help out once school was over. So I think the best plan is to go to my house and wait for him. Maybe I can get my mom to take us to your house, Sam, since it's close to the Tong Offices."

Sam nodded. "Cool."

Maile squirmed. "Sounds great, except…what are we going to have Kimo do?"

I shrugged. "Don't know yet, but I'll figure something out. You two don't have to worry. He's my brother. It was my mistake getting caught, so he's my problem."

We stood and grabbed our things.

"Hey there!" A voice came from the beach.

I glanced from behind a palm.

"Look at this. My two favorite almost-little-sisters and their handsome little friend."

Carly shuffled through the sand toward us.

Iwakaluakumamakahi
(Twenty-One)

I was not even close to being Carly's little sister. Did Maile feel as sick to her stomach as I did? And Sam just looked confused.

"So what are you two sweeties up to?"

Now we were sweeties. I clenched my stomach and pinched my mouth tight. Only an adult like my mom or Mrs. O could call me sweetie.

Sam leaned against a palm trunk, hands anchored in his boardshort pockets. I couldn't tell if he was disgusted with or amused by the little scene taking place in front of him.

"Hi, Carly." Maile smiled, but it looked forced. "What are you doing here?"

"Just had my surfing lesson with your big brother." She beamed and swayed her hips.

I almost gagged.

"Kainoa is simply amazing."

Yeah. He was amazing. But he was pretty dumb not to see through Carly. Man, I wanted to confront her. "Carly?"

She grinned at me and cocked her head. "Yes, Leilani. Oh, by the way, thank you for letting me use your board. That's just so super sweet of you. But, of course, I feel terribly bad you can't surf for almost the whole summer."

I gritted my teeth and tried to smile. "Where were you last night?"

"What?" Her expression faded into a frown.

"Last night, around 12:30?"

She twisted her shoulders and tipped her chin up. "I don't know why you're asking or what business it is of yours, but I was at home asleep. Are you worried maybe I was out late with Kainoa?"

"No."

She marched up close to me. "I think maybe you're jealous. That's it, right? Do you have some sort of little crush on your friend's big brother?" She dug both fists into her waist. "Well, let me clear things up. Kainoa adores me, and he'd never even look at a little twerp like you."

Now I was a little twerp. "Yeah, well, how are you going to explain to your boyfriend that you were out doing criminal activities with two other guys last night?"

Carly's face paled. "I would never do anything against the law. What are you talking about?"

"In the pineapple fields. I saw you and George Hanes and some other guy last night destroying the fruit and plants."

She squeezed her hands into fists and glared. "You're wrong. That had to be someone else. And who's this George guy? Besides, how would you know about what went on in some old field?" She paused and riveted her glare to my eyes. "Unless you were there. But what would you be doing at the plantation in the middle of the night? Don't you know there's a curfew law? Does your mom know you were running around late at night?"

Setting my jaw, I sent Carly a dose of foul-face. "You were there. I saw you, I heard your voice and I confronted the three of you. But you ran off. Why would you vandalize like that?"

She took a heavy step toward me. "I didn't, and you can't prove it."

"Maybe not, since I don't have a picture or anything, but it was you. What do you think Kainoa will say when I tell him?"

"You wouldn't dare. Besides, it's your word against mine. And who's he going to believe? Me, his adoring girlfriend, or you, his little sister's nerdy friend?"

Anger boiled inside. I wanted to strangle her.

Maile moved next to me. "We were there too."

Sam moved to my other side. "Yup. We saw you freaking out and screaming like a little preschooler."

Carly took a step closer. Her breath blasted across my face. "You will not say one word to Kainoa."

Wishing she were far away from me, I stayed silent.

"Got it?" Her hands lightning-quick, Carly shoved me backward. I stumbled and fell on my behind into the sand.

Maile leapt into action, blasting her body against Carly's. "Don't touch my friend, you bully!"

Carly lost her balance for a moment, then raged at Maile. "Your brother would be so mad at you for accusing me of something I didn't do." She pushed her.

I stood and wiped sand from my legs.

Maile was a dangerous opponent when someone made her mad. Her face tight and mouth twisted, she stepped close to Carly and spoke in quiet, controlled words. "We'll see what Kainoa believes when we tell him." She pivoted and stepped away from her enemy.

Too late. Wailing loud and high-pitched, Carly blasted forward like a flying cannonball and slammed into Maile, who smacked head-on into a palm and slid down the trunk onto the sand.

"Maile was right. You're a total bully, Carly Rivers." Sam turned and marched over to Maile.

Groaning, Maile propped herself up against the tree.

I glared at Carly.

Her eyes grew large and she cupped a hand over her mouth.

I waved my cast in her direction. I wanted to smack her with my rock-hard arm, but, somehow, sensible judgment kicked in and I stayed put.

Carly turned and took off running.

Was she shaking as much as I was? I turned and quick-stepped through the sand toward Maile. She held a tissue on her head. I saw blood oozing through. "Oh, great! You may end up with matching stitches to your brother's."

She sighed. "It's not too bad, just got scratched by the rough bark." She pushed herself into a standing position. "Did you see the look on Carly's face?"

I smiled. "We got her, huh?"

Sam clamped both arms across his chest. "Wow, guys. Can't believe you confronted Carly Rivers. She's like the almighty princess around school. Can you imagine what kind of rumors she's going to spread about this whole mess? And what if they make it to the eighth-graders? Man! Every girl in school will probably hate me. I won't have a girlfriend until I'm, like, 25 years old."

I shook my head. "Hadn't thought that far ahead." A shiver crept up my spine. What would Carly say? Would anyone believe us? "You guys, we need to get on this and solve the crime before Carly can do any damage."

"Sounds good to me." Maile brushed herself off and Sam grabbed her pack.

We trucked toward the road, but someone's hollering caught

my attention. I turned and saw a guy running through the sand. His arms waved and sand billowed up all around. As he moved closer, I squinted to see.

"Hey, Leilani. Stop right there!"

Kainoa.

Iwakaluakumamalua

(*Twenty-Two*)

My stomach knotted and my mouth tasted sour. I wanted to slink away, or even better, develop a superpower and become invisible.

Maile sighed. "Oh, man, what's my brother doing here? If Carly already told him what happened, we're in big trouble."

Sam scowled. "How could he know already? She just stomped off in the other direction — unless she's some kind of alien and sent him a telepathic message or something."

"Well, that would explain a lot about her." I shrugged. "Hey, maybe we can send her back to her home planet." I wouldn't have minded flying off to another world right then, myself.

Maile and Sam burst into laughter. At least I had my two friends for protection when Kainoa tried to kill me. I swallowed hard and prayed my wobbly legs wouldn't let me fall down like a lump onto the ground. I had to face him at some point — might as well be now.

Kainoa slowed his mad pace and jogged to a stop.

Holding my breath, I hoped he wouldn't notice any signs of terror on my face or in my eyes.

"Sorry. I didn't mean to yell at you like that, but I was trying to get your attention." He grinned at me. "I wanted to thank you for the warning you gave me at the clinic."

"The clinic?" Maile raised her eyebrows and stared at me.

"Sure." A smile crept across my lips. "But I bet it didn't do much good, huh?"

He nodded. "Yeah, but at least I was able to prepare myself. Dr. Lim nailed me with the whole tetanus shot thing too."

Sam leaned against the palm tree. "What are you guys talking about? Feels like you're speaking in code or something."

"I get it." Wagging a finger, Maile smirked. "You two ran into each other at the clinic." She pointed at me. "When you were getting a new cast." Then a point toward her brother. "And you were getting stitches."

"Yup." Kainoa made an okay sign. "Just wanted to let you know." He turned and ambled through the sand.

Should I tell Kainoa about Carly before he got too far away?

Maile seemed to read my mind. "Hey, wait Kainoa."

"No can, sistah. Gotta help tutu move da kine stuff today."

Maile stood on tiptoe and yelled. "Can't you help Grandma rearrange her living room later?"

He shook his head and waved, then picked up the pace and ran down the beach in a hailstorm of grit.

Hands on hips, Maile scowled. "I hope he isn't heading straight for his girlfriend. She'll, for sure, tell him how mean and evil his little sister and her friends were to her. I can see the tears now."

Yeah. I could see them too. The worst part was the pictures flashing through my mind of Kainoa cradling a sobbing Carly in his arms. Pain shot through my insides. Was I in major trouble or what?

We plodded our way toward my house.

Sam was the bright light in the middle of all the yucky stuff. He prattled on and made me smile. 'Course, it helped that he loved anything sci-fi. "For sure, Carly's an alien, and I figure the people of Earth will kick her into outer space once the leaders find out what she's been doing. Of course, her home planet will be totally angry, 'cause she blew the whole mission and embarrassed them in front of the human race." He waved his hands to the sky. "They'll banish her to a lesser world where all the spoiled brats and snobby princesses end up."

I skipped along, a smile crossing my lips. "I can just see her slapping and clawing at all the other girls, trying to make her way to the top of the heap on Planet Jerk."

Nodding, Sam chuckled. "Yup. Planet Jerk — perfect name for where alien Carly will end up."

Something tweaked my heart. *Sorry, God, for making fun of Carly.* She just made me so mad. I needed to nail her for her criminal actions and stop concentrating on the things she used to do to me and my friends, or on how frustrated I was with her and Kainoa. Yeah, I'd get her for her real crimes.

Sam lumbered beside me. "Have you thought about what Kimo can do?"

"No. Kimo is really smart, he'll know if it's just something to keep him busy. He wants to help for real."

Maile yanked my ponytail. "Think hard, Leilani. We're almost to your house."

I peered between fruit trees and bushes. Squinting, I tried to bring my house into focus. Our car was still in the driveway, so Mom must not have left yet to pick up Kimo. It would give us time to plan. "You guys starving? I am."

"Yeah." Maile nudged me. "You gonna fix us something yummy?"

I nodded and continued to trek forward. Thoughts of Kimo pushed away the horrible visions of Carly with Kainoa. My stomach settled and I concentrated on solving the mystery.

As we hiked up the drive, Mom came out of the house. "Good, you're home. I'm off to pick up your brother."

"Okay, see you later."

"I made some sandwiches, they're in the fridge." She opened the truck door and climbed in. "There's plenty, so help yourselves."

"Thanks, Mrs. Akamai." Maile beamed. "You've saved us from having to eat whatever gunk Leilani was going to fix."

Mom shook her head and focused on me. "Don't forget your phone."

"Got it!" I waved my bag and headed up the stairs.

Inside, Sam headed straight for the fridge.

I deposited my backpack on a chair, opened a cupboard and reached for plates. "Bring all the sandwiches out, Sam. Kimo will be home soon and he'll be hungry too."

Maile grabbed glasses and filled them with iced tea. "Hey, I have an idea. Maybe we could have Kimo get us some shave ice or something while we're interviewing Brody. Wouldn't that make him feel special?"

I frowned at my friend. "No, he'd know we were just trying to get rid of him."

Sam set the huge sandwich plate on the table, grabbed one and sunk his teeth in. "Maybe he could take notes for us during the meeting."

"Yeah, right." I narrowed my eyes. "Sam, you're worse than Kimo with the whole talking-with-your-mouth-full thing. And have you ever seen my brother's scribbles?"

"Worse than yours, huh?"

"Funny." I sighed and ran a finger around the edge of my glass. "Kimo wouldn't think that was important, anyway. He wants to do something exciting, worthwhile and maybe even kind of dangerous."

"Okay, so maybe we should create something that sounds major important." Maile took a huge bite.

"Yeah, but also keep Kimo out of trouble and stop him from irritating us at the same time." I glanced at my friends. "Any other ideas?"

Sam shrugged. "Nope." He downed some iced tea and snatched another sandwich.

After we finished our lunch and dumped our dishes in the sink, the front door opened and I heard Mom and Kimo enter. Mom sauntered into the kitchen, but Kimo dashed down the hall to his room.

"Did you find plenty to eat?"

"Yeah. Thanks, Mom."

She pulled a bottled mocha drink from the fridge. "Hmm. I see you managed to get the dishes to the sink."

"We were going to load the dishwasher next."

"Really?" Mom leaned against the counter, her eyes leveled with mine.

"Yeah." Maile bounced across the floor, Sam tagging behind. "Sam and I will load if you rinse, Leilani."

I turned the faucet and ran a glass under the flow. "How was Kimo's first day of summer school?"

Mom shook her head and popped the cap on the bottled drink. "Don't know, he didn't say much. Seemed a little preoccupied." She glanced at me. "He did want to know if you were home, which I find a little strange."

I shrugged, tried not to look guilty and handed some plates to my friends.

"You two have some big secret going on?"

My heart thumped. Would Kimo ruin our investigation? I twisted my mouth. "Nope. You know Kimo. His imagination is always a little crazy, like he's on some other planet." Could he and Carly be related? I snickered.

"What's so funny?"

"Nothing." I dried my hand and took a step toward her. "We thought we'd hang out near Sam's house. Could you give us a ride over there? You don't have to go all the way to Sam's. The other side of the plantation would be fine."

"Okay, but it's no problem to take you to his house."

Kimo bounded into the kitchen, a baseball cap on his head and a backpack in his hand. He crashed into the chair holding my bag. "I'm ready, Leilani."

"Be careful!" I glared at my brother, then bent over, reached under the chair and rescued the spilled contents.

Mom marched toward Kimo and pulled his cap lower on his forehead. "What are you up to, kiddo?"

"I'm going with Leilani to investigate."

Head cocked, Mom shot me a look that exploded as it hit me. She clamped one hand on her hip. "What is your brother talking about?"

Iwakaluakumamakolu
(Twenty-Three)

I opened my mouth, but no words came out.

Kimo stared at me, his eyes wide and his mouth at half-mast. It seemed he realized he'd blown it for both of us. But then he turned to Mom and put on a giant grin. "Leilani said she'd teach me about The Hawaiian Island Detective Club, you know, how they used to pretend to be detectives and do all that snooping around."

I glanced at Maile and Sam. The fear oozing from their faces seemed to fade.

Mom's vice-grip on her hip relaxed. She shook her head and chuckled. "How could I forget?" She motioned for Kimo to eat a sandwich. "I remember being the subject of many an investigation." She looked up at the ceiling and placed one finger near her lips. "I believe I caught you in my closet spying, as well as in the laundry room." She changed her gaze to me and grinned. "Did I ever tell you how cute you looked trying to hide under a pile of dirty clothes?"

I forced a smile. Did I really do that? Gross!

"Then there was the time you hid in the back seat of the car. Boy, did I get a start when I opened the door to load groceries. And do you remember when you climbed into our mango tree out front? What a mess you were when you fell."

Yup. I must have knocked down every mango on my way to the ground, then landed on top of them. What a squashed mess. How did Mom put up with me?

She continued to tell us stories of my horrible sleuthing while I thought about how to use Kimo to help us today. What was he good at? What would he be willing to do? Then it hit me. He was amazingly good at art for his age, and at observing unique things to put into his drawings. Hopefully, I could convince him that, in order to become a good detective, he needed to practice his observation and sketching skills.

"Hey, Mom, we have to go if we're going to have time to teach Kimo stuff."

"So you're telling me I'd better prepare myself for your brother to take over where you left off?"

"Yup."

"I'll grab my keys and get you sleuths to your crime scene." She snickered.

I glanced at Kimo and spoke soft and low. "Thanks."

He grinned and puffed his chest like a proud peacock.

"Do you have your sketchbook?"

He swallowed a bite. "No. Why do I need it?"

"Just go get it…and your pencils. I'll explain later."

Sam leaned toward me. "Wow! That was close."

I nodded and sauntered out of the kitchen, Maile and Sam close behind.

Maile tilted her head. "So, what's with the drawing pad? You got an idea for Kimo?"

"Yup."

"Let's go." Mom's voice trailed as she headed out of the house.

Kimo blasted down the hall and through the living room ahead of us. Excitement radiated from his entire body.

I hoped my plan would keep him busy and out of our way.

The trip around the fields to the plantation building gave me time to think about the investigation. I was eager to talk with Brody. Should I tell him about George Hanes and how we were wondering if he could be related to Nico? What about Serena? Should I tell Brody we saw him with her?

Kimo sang songs and bounced up and down in his seat. I squeezed my lips into a tight smile as anticipation bubbled inside. I pictured myself doing the same thing as my brother when I was major excited about the detective club. 'Course, I was a teenager now — almost a grownup. I should act more mature than a bopping, nutty kid.

"Here you go, everyone. Is this an okay place to drop you?"

"Sure. Thanks, Mom."

The four of us piled out and waved goodbye.

Kimo pranced around me. "What are we going to do? Who are we investigating? What do I get to do to help?"

"Rule number one, kiddo." I held up a finger. "You have to be calm, no matter how excited or scared you are during sleuthing."

"Okay. I'll try real hard to be good."

Sam pointed toward the building. "Explain the plan while we're walking."

Kimo stood on tiptoes. "Is that where we're going? Are the criminals field workers or something?"

I shook my head. "No. I mean, we don't know. Rule number two. We observe and ask lots of questions, but everyone's a suspect until we have all the clues that point to the culprit."

"Okay. I can do those things. And I'm good at remembering stuff too."

"Good. Maile, Sam and I are going to talk with Brody Trent, one of the Tong Plantation employees. This is important, Kimo. We need you to stay outside the building and draw pictures of the fields."

"What? How's that gonna help?"

"It's your cover, silly. In case someone sees you and asks what you're doing. You show them your art and explain how you love to draw."

"Okay." Kimo stopped walking and squinted at me. "So what am I really doing?"

"You're going to watch everyone who comes into the building. Take notes about them. See if anyone uses a name, and if they do, write it down. Watch for people acting suspicious and maybe try to draw a picture of them. You know, draw the stuff that would help us know who they are, okay?"

He cocked his head. "So you want me to find suspects?"

"Yup. You never know who might be guilty."

"Cool. I can do that." He skipped down the path leading to the building. He found a place under a plumeria tree near the entry and settled onto the shaded grass.

I sent him an okay sign and headed toward the stairs.

Sam poked me in the shoulder. "Glad I don't have a little brother or sister to annoy me to death, but good job with Kimo. How'd ya know what to say to him, anyway?"

Shaking my head, I laughed. "I thought about it for a long time, that's how."

Maile rushed up behind us. "Are we going to ask Brody about Serena?"

"Haven't decided yet, but maybe." I sighed. "Let's check in with the office lady first. Maybe we can find out if Serena is around too."

"Perfect." Maile scurried down the wide hall toward the reception area.

I glanced up at the huge rotating fans. The breeze cooled my face and arms. Ever since I got a cast, my whole body seemed overheated. And now the itching underneath it had started. Drove me crazy. I clenched my teeth and tried to ignore it.

Focusing on the keyboarding woman at the reception desk, I marched forward. "Hi."

She glanced up, peering over the top of the same red-framed glasses. "Hello. Haven't you three kids been here before?"

I nodded.

"What can I do for you?"

"We're here to see Brody Trent."

"Don't you remember where his office is?"

"Yes, but we wanted to ask you something."

She removed the glasses and ran her fingers through the curls hanging around her ears. "Okay."

"Is Serena Tong here today?"

"Do you have an appointment with her?"

"No, but we'd like to see her if it's okay."

"Serena is here almost every day. She's been a great help to her father." The woman smiled. "You'll find her in the lounge around the corner." She pointed, opposite from the hallway where Brody's office was located.

"Thanks." I turned and quick-stepped it toward my friends who had already started toward the lounge.

Before I got far, the receptionist called out to us. "Yoo-hoo, kids!"

I glanced over my shoulder.

"I forgot. Brody isn't in the office today. He's out and about in the fields."

"Thanks."

I caught up with Maile and Sam. They stood still, as if frozen. "What's up?"

They pointed across the large lounge, toward a far wall.

People moved about while others sat at tables, eating or reading. Some seemed to be doing paperwork. Then I spotted them.

Serena was nestled next to Nico on a small couch. He held her hand in both of his. He spoke to her, but we were too far away to hear what he was saying. I wished I could read lips.

I leaned close to my friends and whispered. "Let's sit near them. They don't know us, so we'll be safe."

Sam nodded and trucked along behind me. Maile became the caboose of our little train. By the time we wove between tables, dodged people and settled into nearby chairs, Nico had stood. He leaned down and planted a kiss on Serena's cheek. She didn't look up.

Once he moved out of the area, I stood, motioned for Maile and Sam to follow, and approached Serena.

"You're Serena Tong, right?"

"Yes." She wiped a hand across her cheek, smearing a tear into her hair. "Do I know you?"

I shook my head. "No. I'm Leilani, and these are my friends, Maile and Sam. We know Brody Trent. We met with him the other day."

Her stare bounced back and forth between us. "You kids met with Brody?" She cocked her head. "About what?"

"The pineapple vandals."

She pulled her eyebrows together, wrinkles creasing her nose. "I don't understand. What would you know about the plantation damage?"

Sam jumped on the opportunity to talk. "We don't know anything. That's why we wanted to meet with him. It's about a school project, but that's a way long story. Anyway, Brody was totally cool and met with us, but maybe you could help too."

She smiled. "Okay. Anything to encourage kids on a school project." She narrowed her eyes. "But, it's summer. Why would –"

I waved my hand and shook my head. "Like Sam said, it's a long story, but it's a summer project before we head to eighth grade."

She shrugged. "Okay."

We sat on the sofa opposite Serena. The cotton fabric was soft and cool against my legs. I squeezed into a corner, pulled the notebook and pencil from my backpack, and glanced at Maile and Sam. They probably expected me to take charge and start the questioning. "This plantation is amazing. How long has your family been running it?"

She smiled. "For a number of generations. It's a business my great-grandfather handed down to my grandfather and then to my father. It's something we're all very proud of."

"When we spoke with Brody he said you're the heir to the business."

Serena tucked her hair behind one ear. "Yes. I'm an only child. I've been trying to spend a lot of time with my dad at work, learning about pineapples and running the plantation."

Sam leaned back and laced his fingers together behind his neck. "Tough business?"

Shaking her head, Serena sent a crooked smile in our direction. "Any industry is difficult. The key is to hire the right people."

I bit the inside of my cheek and tapped my pencil on the spiral. "So, what about the damage to the fields? How has it affected everyone?"

"My father's been devastated." She sighed. "He can't figure out why anyone would want to do anything to harm such a thriving plantation."

"Do you think it could be an inside job?"

Serena chuckled. "You sound like a detective — only pint-sized."

I loved how she thought I sounded like a real detective, *but pint-sized?*

Maile waved her hand toward me. "Leilani is really good at this kind of stuff. That's why we picked this as our project. It's going to be the best ever."

I caught Serena's gaze with mine. "So, do you think it could be someone who works here?"

She shook her head. "No. I mean…I guess it could be…but that would be horrible."

How should I ask her about Nico? Would she freak? My throat seemed blocked, and even though I opened my mouth, nothing came out. I swallowed hard.

Serena narrowed her eyes. "I'm sorry. You seem a little upset. Would you like something to drink?"

"No, thank you. I'm okay."

Serena smiled and scooted forward. "Please don't worry. The plantation will survive this little hurdle."

Hurdle? I sensed it was much more. Praying the right words would come out, I opened my mouth. "Do you think Nico Hanes could be involved?"

"Nico?" She shook her head. "How do you know him? And why would you ask such a thing?"

"Brody told us about him. He mentioned he's a local busi-nessman." Glancing down, I noticed my bloodless knuckles and fingertips. I loosened my grip on the pencil and notebook. "He also said Nico is your boyfriend."

Her smile faded and her eyebrows pulled together. "Yes, but I don't understand how any of this is your business. It has nothing to do with the damage to the pineapple crops."

I leaned forward and clutched the top of my notebook. "I'm sorry, but if we're going to do this project well, I need to ask these questions."

She turned her face away and gazed out a window.

I wiped away a drop of sweat snaking along my hairline, swallowed hard and drew in a big breath. How could I ask this? How would Serena react? Did I have the right…?

Shuddering, I opened my mouth and let the words fly. "If Nico is your boyfriend, why would you be secretly meeting Brody at a coffee shop?"

Serena whipped her head toward me, shot a fiery stare and hit the center target in my eyes.

I held her gaze. "And why would you kiss him?"

Iwakaluakumamaha
(Twenty-Four)

"What? I-I don't..." Serena placed both hands on her face. "How would you know about that?"

"Leilani heard you two planning to meet." The words spewed from Sam's mouth. "I mean, she heard it during Brody's phone conversation, so she didn't actually know it was you he was talking to."

He paused about half a second — must have been to think because I'm not sure he even drew a breath. "So we decided to check it out at The Coffee House. That's when we saw you and Brody. We were sitting behind you in a booth, so we could hear you talking."

Waving a hand, Maile jumped in. "But the best part was when you two kissed before you left. 'Course, I missed the whole thing 'cause I was sitting with my back to the entrance, which was all these guys' fault since I had to sit across from them and ended up with my back to the action."

She'd never forgive us.

I glanced at Serena. Mouth hanging open, both brows peaked high above her eyes, she looked like she'd witnessed some horrible event.

Then Sam started in again. "What was up with all that ooey-gooey stuff with Brody, anyway? Seriously, why would you do it? Isn't Nico your boyfriend?"

I held my palm out toward Sam. "Stop! I think Serena gets it."

"My bad. Mom calls me 'Motor Mouth' 'cause...well, you know."

Serena sighed. "So, if you heard our conversation, you know that Nico thinks Brody is behind all the vandalism."

"Yes." I cocked my head. "But what do you think about Brody being involved? Or Nico?"

Her eyes filling with tears, she lowered her chin. "I don't know. It's just so hard for me to think of either of them being involved in such an awful crime against my family."

"Yeah, I understand."

"I don't get it." Sam seemed unable to hold his thoughts imprisoned. They always escaped through his open mouth. "What's up with this whole two boyfriends thing? Just break up with one. Kinda not fair, don't ya think? Seriously, if one of them's a jerk, tell him."

Maile scowled and nudged Sam.

"Sorry. Big-time not my business." Sam frowned. "Guess it's a girl thing. I'll shut up now." He zipped a finger across his lips.

"You're right. It's my business, not yours." A tiny curve stroked Serena's lips. "But I don't want you three leaving here thinking I'm a horrible person." She drew in a deep breath. "I truly love Brody, and he loves this farm. He could never do anything to harm it, and even though my father doesn't recognize his ability to run the plantation, Brody would never hurt him or the business."

Her smile broadened. "I first met Brody Trent when he was out in the fields one day. His eyes were the first things that caught my attention. Not just the brilliant blue color, but the kindness and honesty I could see in them." She paused and looked off into the room. "After that, I found excuses to see him. I'd offer to deliver paperwork from my father to Brody's office and hope he'd be in. I'd wander the fields when I knew he was out working, hoping I'd run into him." She sighed and leveled her eyes with mine. "He's been so good to me, and he's good for my family's farm too."

I shrugged. "But what about Nico?"

"Oh, yes, Nico. You've seen him, right?"

We nodded.

She sighed. "I thought he was the most handsome man on Earth, and so proper — always dressed in a suit and tie. He was smart too. I knew Daddy would love him. Of course, he did, almost the moment Nico walked through the office door." Serena's smile disappeared, leaving stern, tight lips in its place. She swallowed hard. "Nico is the perfect person to take over running the plantation someday."

I tipped my head to one side. "So you're staying with Nico because of your father?"

Serena lowered her chin and spoke quietly. "I don't know what I'm doing. My father adores Nico, and even though he likes Brody, he doesn't think he has what it takes to run this place. Nico is a successful businessman. He'd be so good for our farm. He cares about me and my father. He couldn't ever harm our family's business. It would destroy us."

Sounded to me like she was trying to convince herself, not that she believed it. Was she staying with Nico only because of the plantation's future? Was Brody the true *love of her life?* "Do you know if Nico has a relative, maybe a cousin or nephew or something, named George?"

She twisted her lips and squinted. "I don't think so, but maybe it's somebody I haven't met yet. I'm sure I don't know all of his family members." She leaned forward. "Why do you ask?"

"We think a high school student named George Hanes has some involvement in the vandalism."

Serena shook her head and frowned. "No. I can't believe that person would be related to him. Even though Nico and Brody are very different, neither of them would do this to me or my father."

I stood. "Well, someone is." Reaching my hand toward her, I smiled. "Thank you for sharing with us. And please let us know if anything else happens, or if you think of something that might help us with our inve — our project." I cringed inside, and prayed Serena hadn't noticed what I'd almost said. I wrote my name and number on a piece of paper, tore it from the notebook and handed it to her.

She clasped both hands around mine. "I hope you and your friends realize that what you know about me and Brody is very sensitive." She fixed her gaze on me. "If you say something to anyone else, it could cause a lot of hurt — for me, my father, Nico and Brody."

"We understand."

Maile touched Serena's arm. "I'm so sorry about everything that's happening to your family."

"Thank you." She pocketed the paper I'd given her.

"We wanted to see Brody, but the receptionist told us he's outside working this afternoon." Maile raised her eyebrows. "Do you think you could show us the way?"

"Sure." Serena moved across the lounge and pointed toward a doorway at the end of the hall. "That exit will take you to the back. You'll see a couple of equipment sheds in the fields, and a large storage barn not too far from here. Check those places first. If he's not in one of those buildings, you can try your luck tracking him down in the fields. He could be anywhere." She smiled. "And good luck with your project, kids."

"Thanks." I waved to Serena and the three of us headed out of the lounge, down the hall and through the back door.

The fields shimmered in the afternoon sun. I drank in the smell of ripe pineapple and appreciated the peaceful calm. Rows of fruit stretched for what seemed like forever until they touched the mountains beyond. Two faraway sheds poked up through the deep green pineapple plants. The closer storage barn blended in with the office building — similar colors and construction. Must have been original to the plantation, unlike the odd structures beyond. They were probably built only for storage.

"Wow!" Sam tromped down the stairs. "I've never seen the plantation from over here. Kinda cool. We're always on the ocean side or along the road."

I tipped my head and allowed the rays to penetrate my face. The summer sun was gaining strength every day. Eyes closed, I pictured myself paddling my surfboard like crazy, catching a huge wave and riding it all the way. I tried to control the emotions gurgling inside. Carly had my perfect longboard, and I would never be able to ride a wave this summer. Seriously? Was that even fair?

"Hey, Leilani. What's up?" Maile moved close and wrapped an arm around my shoulders. "You look upset or sick or something."

I gazed at my friend and forced a smile. "Nothing really. Just imagining what this summer might have been like."

"Oh. Why don't you think about what it's going to be like when we nail Carly for this vandalism?"

"Yeah, well, I don't think she knows a lot."

Sam bounded toward a row ahead of us and yelled over his shoulder. "But she was involved, so she's just as guilty."

My forced smile morphed into a real one. "Yeah, that's right." I bumped Maile with my hip. "Let's get going."

She giggled.

"What's so funny?"

"You almost told Serena we were investigating instead of working on a project."

"Sure hope she didn't hear it." I squinted into the sun's bouncing reflections off the storage building. "Let's catch up with Sam."

We darted forward and found him on the far side of the wooden building. "Hey, any signs of Brody?"

Sam shook his head. "Uh-uh. Maybe we should walk around the whole place."

"Okay. Then we'll check out the two far sheds."

Maile stared up at the top of the building. "Wow! This place is so cool. Did you guys see all the neat stuff on the roof?" She pointed to the lacy edging running along the peak.

I adjusted my backpack. "Yeah, it's just like the main offices." Funny how I'd never noticed the fancy stuff before.

We continued to circle the place until we ended up at the door again. I nodded toward the sheds. "Let's try those."

We trekked through the rows, my thoughts drifting back to our conversation with Serena. "What did you think about Serena Tong's explanations?"

Maile shrugged. "I don't know. It seems like she's an honest person, and maybe because of her family's culture, she feels like she has to marry someone her father thinks would be good for the business."

I nodded. "Yeah, exactly what I was thinking."

Sam jogged ahead of us. "Well, I figure it's not a coincidence that George Hanes is involved. Do you know which one of the guys said the thing about the other's relative paying them to do the damage?"

"No." I sighed. "I didn't hear enough of their conversation to figure out who was who, and by the time that George guy came at me with the knife, I was too freaked to pay attention to his voice."

"Yeah, well, I can't believe you walloped him with your cast." Sam's voice faded as he motored further away. Maile and I picked up the pace and caught up with him just as he arrived at the first little shed. It definitely looked deserted. A door was open.

Sam peeked in. "Don't see anyone."

I leaned over his shoulder and Maile peered over the other.

I scrunched my nose. The odor was the same as when I'd open my dad's rusty tool chest. "Ugh! It smells like yucky old wrenches in here."

A demanding voice boomed from behind and made me jump.

"Hey! What are you kids doing?"

Iwakaluakumamalima
(Twenty-Five)

Lunch threatened to escape my stomach. I squeezed my eyes shut and swallowed stale air. How was I going to explain our snooping? Maybe Sam would do some of his famous quick talking and get us out of trouble. Heart thundering against my ribs, I turned around to face the person behind the ominous voice.

"Kainoa?"

He burst into laughter. "You be so da kine scared, yeah?"

I didn't know whether I should be relieved it wasn't some farm worker who would turn us in to the authorities, or super mad he scared me.

"Like my cool imitation of a security guard or something?" He grinned.

Maile swatted her brother. "You are a major jerk. What are you doing here, anyway? You scared us. And, yes, you sounded pretty tough and creepy." She flailed her arms at Kainoa again.

He ducked, then grabbed one of her attacking hands. "I should be asking you three that same question. I was minding my own business driving home from work when I saw Kimo wandering around the fields near the huge plantation building."

"Kimo?" I'd forgotten all about him. He was going to kill me. I should have at least checked in with him before heading outside to look for Brody.

"He told me he was helping you with some kind of project."

"That's right." Good for Kimo. He didn't let Kainoa know about the investigation.

"He said he'd been out there a while and didn't know where you three were, so I volunteered to look for you."

I grinned. "Thanks, Kainoa." I appreciated his help, but even more, I was so happy Carly wasn't with him.

"Let's go. I'll give you all a ride to wherever you want."

Nodding, I smiled and hoped I didn't look all silly and star-struck or something.

Hurrying through the rows, I contemplated what we should do next. "Hey, Sam, can we go to your house and re-group?"

"Sure." Sam trucked along the path, his shaggy hair swishing in rhythm to his determined steps.

I glanced at Kainoa. My hands went clammy and my mouth went dry. I was always nervous around him, but this was different. He needed to know the truth about Carly ... and I should be the one to tell him.

We continued past the storage barn. Kimo rounded the corner of the plantation offices and ran toward us.

"Yay! You found them."

"Hey, little bro!" I ran toward Kimo and gave him a hug. I spoke in his ear. "Thanks for not letting Kainoa know what we were really doing." I messed up his hair. "Sorry about not checking in with you. Time kind of escaped us."

Big eyes and a stupid grin consumed Kimo's face. "I did good, Leilani."

"Yes you did."

"No, I mean I wrote down lots of stuff and drew some real good pictures too."

Squeezing his shoulders, I leaned down and whispered. "You can tell me about it later."

"But…"

We approached the group. "Kainoa's gonna give us a ride to Sam's house."

"Cool."

"Okay, girls, Sam and little Kimo, let's go."

My brother stomped his foot, twisted his face and burst into his best whine ever. "I'm not little. I'm ten years old, and I know lots of stuff and can do things just like Leilani and her friends."

Kainoa laughed and patted Kimo's shoulder. "Sorry. You're right." He ushered my brother toward the old rusted truck and motioned for us to follow. "And you know what? You're also amazingly brave."

"I am?"

"Yup. You told me you were helping these guys with their project, right?"

He nodded.

"Well, I think that's a pretty scary thing. Don't know if I could handle being around three 13-year-olds at once, especially when two of them are girls." Kainoa winked at me. "I'd be afraid for my life."

Kimo laughed and Kainoa gave him a little shove. "Into the truck, big guy."

Once loaded, Kimo looked up at me with bright eyes and a smug, lopsided grin. "Kainoa says I'm brave. That means I'm practically a grownup, just like you."

I squeezed my lips and passed Kimo some evil-eye. I'd never hear the end of it, even though my annoying little brother wasn't even close to being a teenager, let alone an adult. "Yeah, I heard."

Kainoa revved the engine and pulled onto the road. Fruity air wrapped around us through the open windows. "So, what is this project all about and why were you four at the plantation?"

As I'd hoped, Sam dove right in and explained. "We're working on a huge assignment our teacher gave us before leaving school this spring. Eighth grade is a big deal, you know, so she wanted us to be prepared for all the high school prep stuff ahead of us. It's a fun project, 'cause we're supposed to research something really important to our state, or country or –"

"I get it." Kainoa headed Sam off at the pass. "But what's so important about our little local pineapple farm?"

Sighing, Sam tilted his head, lines forming across his brow. "Oh, man, you haven't heard about the damage in the fields?"

"Oh, yeah. Guess I did hear. Bored kids looking for some thrills, right?"

I took the opportunity to jump in. "Could be, but we think it might be something more, so we're researching the whole thing."

"Hmm. And what kind of research were you doing in that old shed?"

I felt my cheeks burn, and hoped Kainoa didn't turn around and see how red they probably were. "We were looking for one of the workers who was supposed to be out there somewhere."

"Wow! So you guys are serious about this, huh?" Kainoa pulled into Sam's driveway. "Here you go, crew."

"Thanks." I piled out of the truck, grabbed Maile's arm, and whispered. "I need to talk with Kainoa."

She frowned. "About Carly?"

"Yeah."

"Are you sure you want to do that?"

Shaking, I nodded. "I have to."

"Okay. Catch you later." She squeezed my arm, a tiny smile appearing on her face.

I rubbed the back of my neck, hoping to stop the throbbing that threatened to build into a major headache. How was I going to approach Kainoa, let alone tell him about Carly? I hated that he spent time with her — an obvious motive for me confronting him with what had happened in the fields. But he had the right to know. If I didn't say anything, he could hate me later on. So, which was better — Kainoa hating me now…or later?

"Kainoa, can I talk with you for a second? I mean, if you have time?"

"Sure." He motioned. "Slide in."

I pulled myself up and settled into the front seat. A piece of torn seat cushion snagged on my shorts.

"So, what's up?"

Shaking, I pulled the vinyl from its grip on my clothes, then gulped hard, hoping to stop the sick feeling inside. Nothing I could tell Kainoa would be as humiliating as throwing up in his truck.

"Leilani?"

The words exploded out of my mouth. "I have something to tell you."

He shrugged and narrowed his eyes. "Okay."

"Last night I was in the pineapple fields, waiting to see if maybe one of the culprits might show up."

"That's kind of a long-shot, don't you think?"

Cocking my head, I shrugged. "Yeah, but I figured it was worth a try." I glued my eyes on him. "Anyway, three people did come."

"Ho, not even! Fo real kine?"

"It's true. Two guys and a girl."

"Did they do damage?"

I focused on my lap. "Yeah."

"So what happened? Did you recognize any of them?"

Clenching my backpack straps in both fists, I tried to look directly at him, but something — probably lunch — was doing gymnastics in my stomach and it performed harder with Kainoa as its audience. Focusing on my lap and concentrating on calming my insides seemed to be the best choice for the moment. "Uh-huh."

"Was it someone you know, from school or something?"

I nodded and locked my gaze on his eyes.

"The girl was Carly."

Iwakaluakumamaono
(Twenty-Six)

"Wot?" Kainoa smiled. "You jokin' me, yeah?"

I shook my head.

He clenched the steering wheel, his white knuckles standing out against his dark tan. "You're wrong. Carly would never be involved in something like that. She's a sweetheart."

I squeezed my lips together and watched as Kainoa's face creased tight with lines. My heart thumped, but not just in fear, pain too. He cared for Carly. How would I feel if someone told me Kainoa was a vandal? I'd be sick inside, and I'd refuse to believe them.

I swallowed hard to get rid of the lump forming in my throat. "I'm sorry."

He glared at me. "If you really are, you'll think about what you saw and realize it couldn't have been Carly with those two jerks."

I stared at him with my mouth open. I'd already apologized, but only because I felt bad for him, not because I was wrong. "Kainoa, I saw her and I heard her. And…"

"And what?"

"I, uh…" Twisting my hands together, I sighed. "I confronted her about it today."

The tension in his face melted a little. "She said it wasn't her, right?"

I shook my head. "No. I mean, she got mad and all, but she didn't really deny it and she basically threatened me if I told you anything." I took in a breath but didn't continue.

"What else? Did she give you a reason or an explanation?"

"No." I held an intent look on Kainoa. "She told me you wouldn't believe me."

His defiant eyes narrowed. "Yeah, well, how else is she supposed to defend herself against your crazy accusations?"

Carly was right. Kainoa was never going to believe me over her. I figured it was time for me to leave before I said something to make him even angrier.

I forced a smile, avoiding his fiery stare. "Thanks for the ride."

"Hey, Leilani!"

I turned toward Kimo's voice. He ran toward the truck from Sam's house.

"What's taking so long? You ever coming inside?" He poked his head through the open window. "I have stuff I want to show you."

"Sorry." I pushed the door open and Kimo moved back. "I think we should call Mom and have her come get you. Maile, Sam and I have some things we need to do." I slid out of the truck.

"Oh, man! I want to help you guys."

"Later, Kimo. After we've had a chance to go over all the evi — the information — for our project." I glanced at Kainoa and prayed he hadn't heard me almost spill the word *evidence*.

Kainoa leaned across the seat. "Why don't I give you a ride home, big guy? That way you won't have to bother your mom."

"That would be fun, Kimo. Go with Kainoa and I'll catch you later at dinner, okay?" I roughed up his hair, leaned down and whispered in his ear. "Don't tell Kainoa about anything."

He grunted and climbed into the truck.

I watched as they drove down the road, Kimo's little hand waving out the window the entire time.

Returning the wave, I sighed. Kainoa would never come near me again, let alone talk with me. Would he confront Carly? Didn't matter. She'd sweet-talk him into believing she was totally innocent and I was crazy.

I trudged toward the house and let myself in the door. "Hey, Sam, Maile!"

Maile's muffled voice came from the back. "In the computer room."

Making my way down the hall, I wished the day would get better. It couldn't get any worse, right?

I approached the room and heard Sam and Maile chuckling over something. I hated to interrupt their fun time, but we had work to do — find Brody and question him, put the evidence together and maybe come up with a theory.

I pushed the door open. "Hey, Kainoa's gone and he took Kimo home."

My friends stared at me.

"What?"

Maile waved her hand around. "Did you tell my brother about Carly?"

I collapsed onto a chair. "Yeah, unfortunately."

"He didn't believe you, huh?"

"Nope."

"I may have to remind my brother about how miserable that Carly Rivers made us when we were in grade school."

"Don't bother. He won't care. All he can see is the perfect girl he's so infatuated with." I sighed. "We have to hope he'll see through her on his own."

Sam nudged me. "At least you told him the truth. He can't ever come back and say you never told him."

"Thanks. I guess that's true."

"Still can't figure the guy out. Kainoa is smart. Why's he so into her? Anyway, who cares about Kainoa and weirdo Carly." A little smirk ran across Sam's face. "What's the next step in the investigation? Who do we talk with or watch next? Where should we do our spying? Does anything make sense yet?"

"Nope, not a thing. But that's why we need to move forward until something clicks."

"You're a totally great detective, Leilani."

"Thanks." I sent Sam a smile. Figured he was trying to make me feel better after the whole Kainoa confrontation thing. Twisting my lips to one side, I eyed my friends. "You two ready to track down Brody?"

Maile jumped up. "You bet!"

"Do you think he might know if George Hanes is a relative of Nico's?" Sam bounced behind me as we plodded down the hall and out of the house.

I led the troops into the pineapple fields. "I'm hoping so. And maybe, if we're really lucky, he'll have an idea who the other guy is too."

"Cool." He darted ahead of me and motioned for us to follow. "Let's get back to the sheds. Brody's got to be around there somewhere."

Sam continued to dodge between the rows of fruit toward the dilapidated buildings.

"Come on, Maile, let's hurry up before he gets too far ahead."

I jogged, Maile tailing close behind.

We managed to catch up with Sam just as he reached one of the shacks. I pushed open the door and stared into the dark void. The only light seemed to be from random sunbeams coming through the cracks in the walls and ceiling. The musty, gross odor hit my nostrils again. I grabbed my nose. "Yuck. Doesn't smell any better than it did earlier."

Before we could move inside, Maile slammed into me from behind and spoke in a lowered, almost panicked voice. "Someone's coming up on the back side of the shed."

I cocked my head and listened — two garbled male voices. I motioned for my friends to follow. We moved to the side of the shed and I inched along the outside wall toward the back. The voices became louder. One of the two men was Brody. I grinned, looked back at Maile and Sam, and sent them an okay sign.

I took a step and opened my mouth to call to Brody, but the other voice spoke before I could. "So, Uncle Brody, what should our next move be?"

Clasping a hand over my mouth, I prayed I was wrong about what I was hearing. Could the talk between the two guys in the fields last night have been about Brody's nephew instead of someone related to Nico? Was Brody behind this whole mess? I clutched my stomach and waited for his response.

"You didn't have much success last night?"

"No. Things were going well until some girl popped up from behind some plants and ruined everything."

Iwakaluakumamahiku
(Twenty-Seven)

"Some girl? Did you recognize her?"

"No. She just came out of nowhere, Uncle Brody."

I motioned for Maile and Sam to stay where they were while I slowly scooted toward the approaching voices. I strained to hear more of the conversation.

"Well, I guess we'll just have to try again."

Brody and his nephew were getting close. I waved at my friends. They must have understood my frantic gesture because both turned and sprinted around the corner to the front of the shed. I dashed after them. Once we reached the entrance, I signaled for them to follow me inside. By the sound of their voices, Brody and his nephew were almost to the front as well. We slipped in around the rusty door just as the two men trudged past the corner. Peeking through a couple splintered boards, I tried to see if I could recognize the nephew as the other male from the pineapple fields, but all I could see was his back and long, shaggy, sun-bleached hair. Nothing looked familiar.

Maile whispered in my ear. "What's going on? Could you hear what they were saying?"

"Yeah." I turned and narrowed my eyes. "And I'm totally bummed about it."

"Why?"

"That guy with Brody." I sighed.

"Yeah?"

"He called him Uncle Brody."

Sam stepped closer. "Got it. You think this nephew is the other guy in the fields last night. You're probably right, 'cause I can't think of another answer. So that means I'm-All-That Brody is a criminal. Too bad for Serena. She seems way into Brody. Now she'll probably have to marry creepy weird Nico just to make her dad happy, and to save the pineapples."

"Thanks a bunch. Certainly makes me feel better."

His mouth listed to one side. "Sorry, Leilani, but that's kinda how it is."

"It's okay. I guess things aren't always what they seem. I learned a hard lesson too."

Maile shuffled toward me. "What?"

"How hard it is to be a real detective, and how easy it is to form conclusions because it's the way you hope things are instead of letting the evidence show you the truth." I thought I'd been open to Brody being involved in the vandalism, but now I realized that, deep inside, I wasn't willing to accept it. Now I was forced to.

My friends stood on each side of me. Maile nudged me. "It's okay, Leilani. You've done a great job as a detective and you can't expect to be perfect — especially the first try."

I smiled. "Thanks, guys. You're the great –"

Bang!

The heavy shed door slammed shut, causing me to jump and swallow the rest of the word. The light in the small building vanished except for the few rays sneaking in through slits in the walls.

Screech! Clunk!

The three of us jumped again. The door shutting was not the result of some random gust of wind. It was definitely the bolt sliding across the door. Pounding footsteps running away from the shed confirmed my fears.

Sam cocked his head and strained to see. "What was that?"

"Someone locked us in."

"Hey! Come back! We're in here." Yelling the entire way, Sam bulleted forward and pounded the door. "Let us out!"

Silence, except for the retreating footsteps. If I could hear the person running, why couldn't they hear Sam hollering?

Maile and I joined Sam. We pounded on the door and shouted. "Help! Please let us out."

I stopped and sunk to the grimy floor, a shiver snaking its way up my spine. "No use yelling."

Maile joined me on the ground. "Why? Don't you think that person can hear us?"

"They hear us."

"Then we should keep on shouting."

I shook my head. "They locked us in here on purpose."

Sam stood over me, arms clamped across his chest. "For real? Why would anyone do that?"

I shrugged. "Don't know, unless…"

"Unless what?"

Sighing, I leaned against some shelves. "What if Brody and his nephew saw us? They could have pretended not to see we were here, then after we slipped inside the shed, one of them — or even both — came back and shut the door."

"But why?"

"I don't know. Maybe to scare us and make us walk away from this whole case."

Sam released the death grip across his chest and dug both hands into his pockets. "Yeah, well, I'd say their plan is working. I'm totally ready to give up."

"Me too." I planted my head against the wood behind me. "Guess I'll have to call my mom. She's going to freak." I searched my bag. "It's not here."

"You sure?" Maile stepped close.

I plowed through again. No phone. "Oh, man! My cell must have fallen out when Kimo knocked my bag over."

Sam groaned. "Great…just great."

Maile stood up and stamped her foot. "Okay, I've had it with you two. Sam, when have you ever been scared of anything? I can't believe this little bump in our investigation would make you give up." She bent over me and wagged her finger in my face. "And you, Miss Dork! You're the queen of The Hawaiian Island Detective Club. This whole thing was your idea, and if we hadn't decided to help, you would have done it all by yourself." She walked around in a little circle. The sparks flickering in her eyes seemed to add light to the dreary room. "So, since Sam doesn't have a cell phone –"

"Thanks a heap for reminding me." He sneered at Maile. "I'm gettin' one at the end of summer. Mom promised."

"And Leilani forgot her cell phone — again, and mine is in a billion little pieces, I say we get up off our behinds and try to figure a way out of here. Afterward, we'll solve this mystery, okay?"

I reached out my arm to Maile. She pulled me up. "Okay, so who has the MacGyver skills?"

My friends laughed and I joined them. It felt good to let go of some of the stress. "Let's see." I glanced around the room. My eyes had adjusted to the darkness and I was able to make out the shelving surrounding us on every wall. They were loaded with boxes and bottles. Above the top shelves, decaying boards still provided slivers of light. Maybe we could break through them, but they were too high. The only spot was the huge door. Could I find something big enough to ram and crash through it? "I have an idea."

Sam sighed. "Good, 'cause I'm getting way hungry. My mom's going to wonder what happened to me. Usually by this time, I'm bothering her about dinner."

"Yeah. I'm a little hungry myself." I walked toward a group of tools and pointed. "Look for something we could use to break down the door."

Maile cocked her head and planted both hands on her hips. "You're kidding, right?"

"No. Let's try it."

"I don't think we're strong enough, except maybe Sam. But he can't bust the thing by himself." She panned the area, raised her palms and shrugged. "Besides, I don't see anything big enough or thick enough to do any damage to that humungous door."

I sighed and dug through the tools. Most were for gardening, probably for keeping up the grounds around the plantation buildings. I pushed them aside and peered into the dark corner. "Here we go. This might work."

Sam bounded up behind me. "That thing looks huge. Maybe we can lift it and get enough power to bust through the door. Then we'll be heroes. Besides, if we don't go for it, no one will come by for hours –"

"Or days." I pulled on the thick, heavy board and dragged it into the center of the room.

"Good job, Leilani." Sam slapped me on the back. "I'm sure this will work. Gross! What is it?"

"Not sure. Maybe a fence post." I gripped the end of the wood. "This thing is really old and ragged. If we try to use it, I think we'll get a ton of slivers."

Maile made her way to some shelving and grabbed a bunch of rags. "Cover your hands with these. It should protect us."

"Great idea." I wrapped a thick layer around my right hand and left fingers. Maile and Sam did the same. "Okay. Now I'll get the end and you two grab the middle section. Then we'll ram it into the door."

The three of us lifted the makeshift battering ram.

"On three, we'll go for it." I sucked in a deep breath. "One… two…three!"

We lunged toward the door and blasted the wood into the center. Our weapon bounced back as if the door was made of rubber, dropping me onto my rear end. Maile and Sam fell, too, and the huge board landed between them, onto my leg.

"Ouch! That hurt."

Maile crawled toward me and pulled the heavy piece of lumber off. "Oh, man, Leilani. Don't go and break your leg now."

"Believe me, that's the last thing I want to do." I rubbed the injured spot. "Bet I'll have a huge bruise."

For a moment, we were silent. Then Sam burst into a deep belly-laugh. Maile and I joined him. Pushing myself backward with one hand, I slid on my behind and rested against a stack of boxes. "I can't believe we're laughing when we're in such a stupid situation."

Maile sighed. "Somebody will miss us, eventually."

Sam cringed. "I hate the dark, especially in such a gross, smelly place."

"It won't be dark for a few hours." I stood and maneuvered

toward some shelves. "Maybe there's a flashlight in here some-where."

"Hope so."

I prayed I would find a light of some kind to help Sam with his anxiety. He'd hated the dark for as long as I'd known him. "While we're waiting to be rescued, why don't we tell some jokes or funny stories?"

"Great idea." Maile stood and rummaged through stuff on some shelving in another area. "I'll tell the first one." She shared her story and we all laughed, I found an old flashlight with batteries that actually worked, and Sam seemed to be back to his old positive, talkative self.

The sunlight still peeking in under the door was partially blocked by a shadow. We fell silent. Someone stood outside the shed.

Iwakaluakumamawalu
(Twenty-Eight)

The metal bolt screeched as the unknown person slid it open. I shivered, realizing that our rescuer could be the same person who'd locked us up. We might be in danger. The door squeaked open.

"Leilani, you in there?"

"Kimo! Yes, we're here."

My little brother popped through the opening, a grin all over his face.

Maile jumped up and down while Sam whooped. Then came the high-fives.

I shuffled toward Kimo. I kinda wanted to give him a huge hug, but I was more curious about what was going on. "What are you doing here?"

"I knew you were in trouble or something when you were gone so long, so I came to rescue you." He lunged forward, performed a couple martial arts moves and laughed. "Cool, huh?"

"Does Mom know you're out running around? And how did you get here, anyway?"

He shook his head. "Don't worry. She's busy making dinner. I told her you were planning on staying a while at Sam's house and his mom was bringing you home, so she's not worried about you. She thinks I'm out riding my bike, but I didn't say I was coming here to look for you." He smirked. "Now you have to let me help you some more, Leilani, 'cause I know two secrets about you."

I sent him a fiery stare. How did Kimo end up so involved in my investigation of this mystery? I sighed. "Guess I do owe you since you saved me." I rubbed his head and messed up his hair. "Thanks."

"Oh, wait, I have some stuff to show you." He retreated out the door toward his bike. We followed. He tugged at the sketchbook anchored behind the seat.

"What do you have?"

"Some stuff I wanted to tell you about this afternoon, but you wouldn't let me." After releasing the thick pad from bondage, he opened it. "I drew pictures of the people I saw and I wrote some things down, just like you said."

Kimo's drawings were simple, but he did a good job of adding the details needed to recognize the people. The first picture was of Brody. I could tell by the baggy pants and short, cropped hair. "Hey, good drawing. That's the guy we were looking for." I groaned. "And now it looks like he's probably behind the damage in the pineapple fields."

"Really?"

I nodded. "What else you got?"

Kimo flipped a page.

Sam and Maile scooted in close to see the drawings.

"This guy came by later." He pointed to a young man in his drawing.

I didn't recognize him, but Kimo had drawn him with shoulder-length, shaggy hair. Could have been Brody's nephew.

He turned the page. "Then this guy came out of the building."

Maile jumped up and down and wagged her finger at the page. "Look! That's Nico Hanes. See the tie Kimo drew? And it looks like he's wearing a suit."

Kimo flipped to another page and read his scribble. "Yeah. That first person asked the man if he knew where Brody Trent was."

"Are you sure?"

"Yup. I wrote it down."

"Flip back to your drawing, Kimo." He turned the page. I grabbed the book, held it close and stared at the younger man.

Maile strained to see the drawing close-up. "Leilani, is that the second guy you saw in the fields last night?"

I concentrated on the figure Kimo had sketched. My brother was a terrific artist, but nothing he drew reminded me of the other vandal. "No, it doesn't look like the creep damaging the fields. It could be Brody's nephew, but I don't know."

Kimo reached for his book. "I have more pictures and writing." He turned the page. "This is the same guy who came out of the building. He walked around a little bit, and then this person right here…" He pointed to another man in the drawing who was with Nico. "He came over and started talking with him."

"Oh, my!" I stared at the baldheaded man with a scruffy beard.

Maile squeezed my arm. "What is it? Do you know him?"

"No. I mean — I don't know his name or anything, but I recognize him."

"Who is he?"

"The man who met Nico at the medical clinic. Kimo, did you hear what they were talking about?"

"Yeah." He flipped the page, stared at his messy notes and pointed at Nico. "The first man told the other guy he was almost ready to run the plantation." He paused and squinted. "Then he answered and said it was good and he'd start planning...um... the sale."

"What?" Maile clamped a hand over her mouth.

Sam shook his head. "Nico's a total creeper. We should tell Serena so she doesn't marry the jerk. What a bummer for the plantation to be sold to some big corporation. We have to stop it. Let's get on this now and tell Serena."

I waved a hand in front of Sam. "Slow down."

"Why? This is a huge break in the case. We gotta move fast."

"Yeah, well, we still have a whole bunch of questions to answer."

Maile chimed in. "Like, what is Brody's involvement, and his nephew's too?"

I sighed. "If the guy in Kimo's drawing is Brody's nephew, why didn't I recognize him as the second guy in the group from last night?"

Sam shrugged and stuffed a hand in a pocket. "Okay, I get it."

"It's getting pretty close to dinnertime, Sam. How about we meet tomorrow at your house and then track down the two of them at the plantation?"

Maile frowned. "Yeah. I bet my mom is going to kill me for not being home in time to help with dinner."

I shoulder-nudged her. "Your mom is pretty cool. You always worry, but she hasn't killed you yet."

"Yeah, well, when she grounds me from everything, I might as well be dead."

Sam yanked Maile's arm. "Come on, let's get back to my house. You can call her from there. Besides, I'm about to starve to death." He turned toward me. "You and Kimo can come too."

I shook my head. "Thanks, but I'll just ride on the back of Kimo's bike. My house isn't too far away if we're on a bike." I glanced back at the building that had imprisoned us, and cocked my head. "We forgot about one of the biggest questions."

Maile twisted her mouth. "Really? What?"

"Who locked us in this shed?"

Kimo clipped the sketchbook onto his bike. "I have an idea."

"You do?" My brother didn't know enough about the case to have a clue who locked us in that grungy place.

He shrugged. "Well, maybe. I saw a guy walking away from here when I was riding to the big building. I watched him for a while until he went to the parking lot and drove away. I looked around for you guys, but when I couldn't find any of you, I decided to go look around that big barn and these little buildings. When I got close, I heard your voices. That's how I found you." He beamed.

How did Kimo's job go from being a meaningless assignment to super important? He knew two secrets about me and now he'd helped out the investigation big-time. Would I have to let him in on everything I do for the rest of my life? I sighed. "Did you draw a picture of the man?"

"Nope."

Good! He'd made a mistake. Didn't want Kimo to be the better detective. I glared at him. "Why not? It would have really helped."

"Didn't need to."

I narrowed my eyes and folded both arms across my chest.

"It was that guy in the pictures — the one in the fancy clothes who was coming out of the plantation building."

Iwakaluakumamaiwa
(Twenty-Nine)

Nico Hanes. He must've been the one who locked us in the shed, but why? How would he have known we were even out here?

Maile and Sam waved and headed toward Sam's house. Settling in behind Kimo on the bike, I thought about our crazy day. I tipped my head back, pulled the band from my ponytail and allowed the breeze created by the ride to blow through my long hair. The whole pineapple mystery was very complex, but maybe the answer was close.

Kimo pedaled hard and managed to keep us moving fast, even with the extra weight. I grinned at the thought of him madly drawing and writing. He was a little trooper to come find me and my friends. His observation skills were amazing, and he was so excited to be part of the investigation. I had to admit that he was a good detective, but he'd end up doing something stupid at some point. Then I could use it against him. No need to worry about him nosing his way into my business all the time, but I'd for sure give him another chance to help with investigating. My mouth curved and I soaked up the warm evening's rays.

"Thanks, Kimo."

He huffed out the words. "It's okay. I can make it."

I wiped a renegade hair from my face. "Yeah, thanks for letting me ride home with you, but what I really meant was, thanks for helping so much with our investigation."

"Cool." He groaned a little with each push of the pedals.

Maybe Mom's comment about Kimo being a special blessing from God kinda made sense now. He definitely irritated me, but how else could he get my attention? I pretty much ignored him all the time. Who'd have known my little brother would rescue me and my friends, and give us some super-great clues to the pineapple fields mystery? My lips stretched into a smile.

Kimo stopped pedaling and dug his feet into the ground. "Can we walk the rest of the way?"

"Sure." I climbed off the bike.

"Did I really do good, Leilani?"

"Yup. Not only did you rescue me, Maile and Sam, but you gave us some great evidence too."

"Do you know who ruined the pineapples?"

"Not for sure, but we'll find out tomorrow."

"Me too? Can I come? I'm a good detective. I can help some more."

I shook my head. "Sorry, kiddo, but you have summer school, remember?"

Kimo's mouth dropped into a frown. "Man, that's not fair."

I put my free arm around him and squeezed. "Let's hurry. We only have a couple blocks to go, and Mom's going to wonder where you are. Besides, I'm hungry."

"Me too." His face still sported a frown.

"Tell you what. We'll be sure to give you credit for your help in the investigation. You'll be super important."

His frown morphed into a tiny smile. "Okay."

The familiar lanai and surrounding greenery loomed ahead. We trudged toward the side of the house where Kimo propped his bike against the wall. After snatching his drawing pad, he stomped up the stairs ahead of me and raced into the house. "Hi, Mom. I'm back."

"About time, mister. I was almost ready to jump in the car and start looking for you."

I slipped in through the door and stood next to Kimo.

"Leilani." Mom clamped her hands on her hips. "Where have you been all afternoon? I called Luana, but she said Maile was out with you and Sam."

I fixed my eyes on her and opened my mouth to answer.

"And what did I tell you about remembering your cell? I tried to call you and heard it ringing from the kitchen floor."

"I guess it fell out when Kimo dumped my bag."

"Don't blame Kimo again. You were the one who left your backpack on the chair, and when it fell you should've made sure you picked up everything, especially your phone." She drew in a big breath. "I have your phone now and will keep it until I feel you're ready to handle the responsibility."

I frowned. "But, Mom!"

She clamped her arms across her chest and stared.

I groaned. Kimo had saved us, but we wouldn't have needed rescuing if he hadn't spilled my stuff in the first place. 'Course, then I would have had to call Mom and she probably would have freaked big-time — more than she did about me leaving my phone. I sighed. Kimo had won again, and now my phone was being held captive.

Mom shook her head and waved a hand. "Now get washed up. Dinner is ready." She turned and plodded into the kitchen.

Relieved she didn't wait for an explanation about the late

return, I hustled toward my room.

Kimo trotted beside me. "Man, that was close. Aren't you glad I found you guys?"

I sighed. "Yeah." I stopped and bulleted him a piercing stare. "And it's our secret, okay?"

"I won't tell Mom." He beamed. "Detectives have to stick together, right?"

I clenched my teeth and squeezed my hands into fists. "Yeah." My brother was going to hold the night in the pineapple fields and the afternoon in the shed over my head forever. How messed up was that? Special blessing? Yeah, right. Sighing, I tipped my head back. *Sorry, God.* I turned and marched into my room.

After a quick wash-up, Kimo and I slipped into our chairs at the table.

Mom joined us and passed the food. "So, what did you, Maile and Sam do today?"

I swallowed the lump forming in my throat. "We worked on our project."

"Project?"

"Yeah. It's something we're researching."

"And what would that be?"

I slurped up a long spaghetti noodle. Sauce dribbled down my chin. A napkin came in very handy. "The vandalism at the pineapple fields. We've been talking with some people who work there."

Lines spread across my mom's forehead. "You have? How did you manage that?"

"Remember the guy driving the truck we almost hit?"

She nodded.

"I called him and he let us interview him."

Mom smiled. "Very resourceful, Leilani. I'm glad you're doing something meaningful instead of sitting around thinking about boys or lamenting the fact that you can't surf."

Boys and surfing — did she have to bring up those two things? Kainoa and my surfboard hadn't been on my mind in quite a while. I clenched my fork hard as a little movie in my head showed Carly on my beloved board. Stomach panging, I pictured her holding hands with Kainoa. The worst thing of all, though, was seeing Kainoa gazing at her with goofy, adoring eyes.

I dropped my fork onto the table.

Mom cocked her head. "You okay, Leilani?"

"I don't know. My stomach kind of hurts. May I be excused?"

"Of course. Why don't you lie down a while and I'll check in with you later."

Nodding, I pushed away from the table. The thought of shoving one more bite of food into my mouth made me nauseous.

I entered my room and collapsed onto the bed. The visions raged in my mind. How was I going to stop them? Pictures of Brody, Serena and Nico joined the others. Who was guilty and why? It seemed that Nico was planning to marry Serena, take over the plantation and then sell it to someone else. But why would he want to sabotage the fields he would one day own?

Brody's nephew saw me in the fields last night. He didn't look like the second guy I saw. Was he a fourth person involved in the vandalism? Maybe he arrived late and I just didn't see him because of the confrontation. But why would Brody destroy the fields that would one day belong to the woman he loved?

Before I could figure out what to do next, my mom poked her head in the door. "Leilani, you have a phone call."

"Thanks, Mom." She approached and I took the receiver.

"Leilani, this is Brody Trent."

I shuddered. "Oh, yes."

"I think you need to come by my office tomorrow so we can talk again." He sighed. "I know you were in the pineapple fields last night."

Kanakolu
(Thirty)

The phone bounced against my ear in time with my shaking hand. "You do?"

"Yes. In fact, you might want to bring your friends by as well. Would you be able to come to the plantation during my lunch hour tomorrow, about noon?"

Brody's voice floated through the receiver, calm and in control – not at all scary or mean. Still, I worried. Why did he want to meet me? He wouldn't hurt me in his office, would he? He could threaten me. Would I be able to stand up to this man who was possibly behind the scheme to destroy the pineapples and the business?

"Leilani?"

"Oh, I'm sorry." I tilted my head back, stared at the ceiling, then cringed. "Okay, of course. I'll — we'll meet with you tomorrow."

"Great. See you around noon."

The phone dropped to my lap and I fell backward into my pillow. What had I just agreed to? Maybe I'd be safe with Maile and Sam there. He couldn't possibly take on all three of us at once. But if his nephew was there, we'd be in trouble for sure.

I sighed, picked up the phone and punched in Maile's home number. When she answered, I must have sounded sad.

"Okay, Leilani. What's wrong? Out with it."

I swallowed hard. "You'll never guess who just called me."

"Uhhh…Carly? Sorry. Couldn't resist."

"Yeah, well, I could have done without the reminder."

"So, who?"

"Brody Trent."

"What? I mean, why?" She groaned. "For real?"

"Yup. He wants to meet with me tomorrow during his lunch time."

"But, why?"

I rolled to the side and propped my elbow into the soft pillow. "You won't believe this, but somehow he figured it out."

"Figured what out?"

"I was in the pineapple fields last night."

"Yeah, right. How would he know?"

"I don't know. Maybe his nephew identified me from a picture."

"Okay." Maile paused for a moment. "So, are you going?"

"Of course." I swallowed hard. "And so are you."

"Oh, man! You may not be afraid, but I'm terrified. What if he tries to hurt us?"

"I don't think we'll be in danger. He invited you and Sam to come. And it's at the plantation, so I'm pretty sure nothing bad will happen there." I rubbed my head. "Except…"

"Except what?" Maile's voice raised a pitch or two.

"He could threaten us."

"Oh yeah. Nothing to worry about, huh?" She screeched, then shouted into the phone. "Leilani, what have you gotten us into?"

"I'm sorry. But we're so close to solving this case. I really feel we need to go meet Brody tomorrow. I don't think he knows we overheard him and his nephew talking, so maybe he just wants to lecture me about being away from home and in the fields so late at night."

"I guess you could be right." After a moment of silence, she groaned. "Okay, I'm in."

"Great! I'll call Sam and explain the situation to him too. I'll meet you in front of the plantation tomorrow at noon."

After calling Sam and going through the same process with him, I picked up the house phone, plodded down the hall and replaced it on the base.

The sweet scent of baking apple pie wafted from the kitchen. I poked my head around the corner and sucked in the delicious smell. "Yum, Mom. You making a pie?"

She wiped her hands on a towel and smiled in my direction. "Yes. In fact, I wanted to talk to you about tomorrow." She opened a cupboard and pulled out her recipe file. "We're having a big luncheon for all the ladies at church. I'm baking pies tonight, and tomorrow I'm helping set and decorate the tables." She plowed through the multitude of cards. "Where is my Lemon Cake Pie recipe?"

"Do you need help with the baking?"

"Ah ha! Here it is." She pulled out a card and plopped it on the table. "That would be wonderful, sweetie, but I mostly need help tomorrow. I have to pick up flowers, vases, candles and tablecloths. Then we have to organize place-settings, arrange flowers and decorate, not to mention preparing the long serving tables."

"You need me to help?"

"Yes I do. The luncheon is at 1:00."

I cringed.

"So any plans you have with your friends will have to wait until after that."

Kanakolukumamakahi
(Thirty-One)

The next day I dragged myself out of bed at o'dark-thirty in the morning. It wasn't actually dark outside, but still felt like the middle of the night. Getting up early was the only way I could convince Mom to let me off church luncheon duty at 11:30. The biggest challenge was getting to the plantation, but I'd called Maile again last night and she got Kainoa to agree to pick me up at the church and drive us to the offices. Man, I dreaded seeing him. I doubted he'd say one word to me.

I shuffled to the bathroom, but before I made it into the shower, someone banged on the door. "Yeah?"

It creaked open and Mom yelled. "We're leaving in 20 minutes."

"Okay, almost ready." Not exactly true, but I could kick it into high gear.

After a quick shower, I slipped into shorts and a favorite tank-top. I hustled into the kitchen with enough time left to eat breakfast.

"Good morning. I fixed a bagel and cream cheese for you." Mom nodded toward the table. "Our first stop this morning will be the florist. Afterward, we'll pick up vases and linens."

"What about Kimo? How's he getting to school?"

Mom slipped a pie into a carrier. "The lady who launders and presses all the tablecloths lives near the school, so we'll drop Kimo at his class after picking up the linens."

"So he's coming with us?"

Mom glanced at the clock. "Yeah. I'd better check on him. He wasn't too excited about getting up so early this morning."

I chomped on my bagel while Mom battled Kimo. He definitely fought the getting-up-early thing. I chuckled at his shrill whine.

Mom won, though, and soon we were heading out the front door and into our SUV.

First stop, the florist shop. I loved the sweet scents and bright colors. While Mom chose the floral combinations, I admired every beautiful lei in the cold case. My favorite was the pink plumeria.

It seemed every tourist in Hawaii received a lei when they arrived at the airport or when they attended a luau, but not me. I frowned. Didn't seem quite fair since I'd lived on the islands my entire life. Maybe Mom would give me one when I turned 16.

I sighed — another reason to wish I was 16 instead of 13.

"Leilani?"

I forced my gaze away from the leis and toward Mom.

"What do you think of these colors together?" She held up some red Birds of Paradise with white and purple orchids.

"Perfect."

The tropical blooms filled the car with bright colors and amazing smells. After picking up the flowers, vases and linens, we dropped Kimo at school. Next stop, the church.

Nerves seemed to take control as my heart thumped hard with every passing minute. The noon meeting worried me.

Loading and unloading stuff kept my anxiety under control. I worked hard and fast to get as much done as possible before leaving. What if Mom panicked about finishing, and changed her mind about letting me leave early?

The wall clock showed 11:29. I placed tea lights on the last table and stepped back to admire my work. Trekking across the room, I waved to Mom. "Bye, I'm leaving. See you later this afternoon."

She waved. "Thank you for all the help. Your tables look gorgeous."

Loving the compliment, I beamed while exiting the church.

Kainoa's truck approached and Maile leaned her head out the window. "Hey, come on. Let's go."

I quick-stepped across the sidewalk and grabbed the truck door handle. Maile squeezed close to her brother and I hoisted myself up and onto the seat.

Kainoa checked his mirrors and maneuvered onto the street. We rode in silence for a while. I wondered if Kainoa still hated me for what I'd told him about Carly. Finally, he broke the silence. "What are you two girls doing this afternoon?"

Maile looked at me and raised her eyebrows.

I swallowed hard and forced out the words. "Still working on our summer project researching the pineapple plantation and all the vandalism."

"Thought you'd be way done with all that."

I sighed.

"By the way, Leilani, I asked Carly about the other night. She said she would never do such a thing, and you are wrong about seeing her." He glanced at me, then fixed his eyes on the road. "Carly's a sweetheart, and she wasn't mad or anything. She feels sorry that you have to give up surfing all summer and is sure the pineapple vandalism is a substitute. Figures maybe your imagination has gone a little wild."

I had to button my lip, afraid I might say something horrible.

Maile turned toward her brother. "Leilani is not imagining. You can choose to believe Carly if you want, but someday you'll find out what a jerk she is."

Kainoa pulled the truck to the office building entrance. "Man, you girls are both crazy. Get going and do your stupid project."

We piled out of the truck, closed the door and moved toward the entry stairs.

Kainoa yelled out the window. "And leave Carly and me alone." He gunned the motor and the clunky truck rattled away, leaving behind a puff of gray, stinky smoke.

"Wow! My brother is totally blind when it comes to Carly."

"Yeah. How sad is that?" I sat on a stair.

Maile sighed and plopped herself next to me. "He'll be so hurt when the truth comes out." She nudged my shoulder. "And it will come out, Leilani, because you're going to solve the mystery."

I smiled at her. She had such a positive outlook on everything. "I guess we're early."

Maile craned her neck. "Yeah, but I think I see Sam's mom's car coming down the road."

"Cool." I placed an arm across my stomach and leaned forward in an attempt to stop the fluttering inside.

The car coasted to a stop. Sam jumped from the passenger side and jogged toward us. "Hey! How long you been here? Am I late? You guys creeped out about this meeting? Kinda weird that Brody knew about our stakeout. What's up with that jerk, anyway? It's like he turned into a total nutcase. Don't get how he could destroy all those pineapples."

Sam's brain sped like a racecar in high gear. I grinned and shook my head. "No, you're not late, and yes, I'm nervous."

Maile nodded. "Me, too, for sure."

I stood and turned toward the door. "We have to find out the truth, and maybe it will happen today." Blasting out a big breath, I took a step. "Let's do it."

We marched into the building and down the hall toward Brody's office. My insides still raged, and now my hands shook. What would happen? What would we find out? "Here we go."

Brody's office door was open about halfway. I could see him working at his desk. I knocked.

He looked up and then stood. "Leilani, come on in."

I pushed the door, took a step into the office and froze.

Brody's nephew stood in the corner.

Kanakolukumamalua
(Thirty-Two)

I recognized his hair — the light, sun-bleached color and the long, shaggy cut — just like the picture Kimo drew of the person asking for Brody Trent's office.

Brody motioned. "Come on in. I'm glad all three of you are here. I want you to meet someone." A slight smile crossed his lips as he swept an arm toward the teen in the corner. "This is my nephew, Drew. He's the reason why I'm sure it was you in the pineapple fields the other night, Leilani."

I trembled.

He maneuvered to the front of the desk and hiked one hip onto the edge. "Drew, is this the girl you saw?"

"Yup."

Brody tucked both arms across his chest. "I figured it had to be you because of our conversation the other day." He narrowed his eyes. "Be honest with me. This is *not* about some school project, is it?"

I stared at my toes and shook my head.

"You're investigating and trying to solve the mystery of who's damaging the pineapple crops, right?"

Looking up and locking eyes with Brody's, I let a flood of words escape. "Why was Drew in the fields the other night?

Are you part of this whole vandalism thing? I don't understand why you would be doing this. Does it have to do with Serena and Nico? Is it true maybe you're looking for work at another plantation? Or –"

"Whoa! Hold on." He shook his head and chuckled. "You're pretty good at this investigating thing, but you don't have all the facts." He nodded toward his nephew. "Drew was also investigating the other night. The farm can't afford to hire professional security, so I asked him if he'd be willing to help. He wasn't part of that group of vandals. He was hiding in the fields, just like you. Somehow you two never ran into each other."

Drew nodded. "Yeah. I was shocked when you stood up and yelled. I kept a close eye on the confrontation, and was about to tackle that guy who had the knife when you took care of him with your cast." He grinned. "Pretty gutsy."

"And *that*, Leilani, is why I was sure it was you in the fields. The cast." Brody smiled.

I closed my mouth. I figured it must have been hanging open during the entire explanation. Maile and Sam stared with wide eyes and open mouths too.

Brody, still propped against his desk, uncrossed his arms and gripped the edge. "The bad news is, we still don't know who's doing the damage. I'd hoped Drew would recognize someone if they were teens, but they must all attend public school. Drew goes to a private one, so nobody looked familiar to him."

My lips parted and a smile spread across my face. "I think I can help."

"Okay." Brody narrowed his eyes and cocked his head. "Tell me what you've got."

I swallowed hard. "First of all, one of the boys smashing the pineapples said something about the other one's uncle paying them to do the damage. The next day I found one guy's picture in the school yearbook — George Hanes. Even though I can't prove it, I think he must be Nico's nephew, which would make Nico the uncle paying for the job." I winced and glanced at Drew. "Sorry. I thought you were the nephew involved, and your Uncle Brody was the culprit behind this whole mess."

Drew passed me a crooked smile. "No problem. I understand how you could come to that conclusion, but how did you know he was my uncle?"

My cheeks burned. "Well...we overheard you talking with Brody in the fields near the shed yesterday."

Brody shook his head. "No wonder you were confused. I'm sure our conversation made us look very guilty."

I nodded toward Drew. "The only problem was, you didn't look like the second guy in the fields. We've never figured out who that person was. Some random friend of George Hanes, I guess." I smiled and focused on Brody. "I'm so happy you're not involved."

"Thanks. Now go on with your story."

"Anyway, my brother, Kimo, is a great artist, so he helped us yesterday by drawing pictures of everyone he saw going in or out of the plantation. He also wrote down as much as he could of what people said. One of those pictures was Nico Hanes talking with some man. And because Kimo drew him with a bald head and a beard, I'm sure that person was the same one Nico met with at the medical clinic a couple days ago."

Brody cocked his head, creases forming on his forehead. "I don't –"

"I was getting a new cast because my first one got soaked." I sighed. "Anyway, not important. Nico said he was there to get allergy shots and figured it would be a great place to meet."

Shifting his weight, Brody scowled. "What did they say?"

"At the clinic, something about getting everything in place and the timing had to be right. Also something about the other man writing up a proposal."

"A proposal for what?"

"I didn't have a clue, but Kimo overheard Nico yesterday telling the same man he was close to owning the plantation. Then the other guy said he'd work on the sale."

Brody hung his head. The silence hovering throughout the room throbbed in my brain. What was Brody thinking? Did he believe me? I decided to break the cold quiet. "I'm sure Nico was the one who locked us in the shed yesterday too."

"What?"

"We'd ducked into the building when we heard you and Drew talking. After you left, someone shut the door and slid the bolt. I thought it was you until Kimo told me he saw Nico heading from the shed toward the offices. My brother was the one who saved us."

"Wow! You three have been through a lot."

I shrugged. "I guess, but now I want to solve this whole thing. I want to confront Nico."

"No, Leilani, not without help." Brody glanced at his watch. "It's lunchtime and Nico usually comes by to eat with Serena. We can question and maybe even challenge him together."

My heart pounded. "Yeah, let's go for it."

We trudged down the hall, Brody in the lead. He took us to the lounge where we'd first talked with Serena. A hum of voices tickled my ears as I peeked around Brody. Nico and Serena were seated nearby, eating lunch.

We wove around a few tables and approached the couple, Brody speaking first. "Nico, we need to speak with you." He turned and wrapped an arm around my shoulder. "Actually, Leilani will do the talking."

Nico's eyebrows pulled together into a frown. "What's this all about? Serena and I are trying to have a peaceful lunch here and you're interrupting. Make an appointment with my office." He turned his gaze back to Serena.

I took a step forward. "No, Mr. Hanes. We will talk right now." My legs turned limp, like soggy noodles. They wobbled. *Lord, give me the right words.* "Sir, we know you're behind the pineapple fields vandalism. We're not exactly sure why, but my guess is that you're trying to discredit Brody Trent in order to keep Serena under your control." I glanced at her.

She fixed her gaze on Nico. "Nico?"

"You paid your nephew, George, and his friends to damage the crops. You accused Brody and spread rumors that he was looking to work at another plantation and trying to destroy the Tong farm."

"Absolutely not true."

"Yes it is." I motioned toward Maile and Sam. "The three of us overheard you yelling and saying these things to Brody the first day we met with him." I swallowed hard. "It was your plan to marry Serena, gain control of the plantation and sell it to a larger corporation."

"Your accusations are absurd. I would never hurt Serena and her family."

"Yes you would. You have been overheard twice making plans with some other man who is probably from another plantation."

"What? Where are you getting such insane information?"

"A couple days ago at the medical clinic, and yesterday in front of this building. My brother drew pictures of the two of you. I'm sure Brody can figure out who it was and which farm they're from."

Nico stood and slammed his chair against the wall. "You kids are crazy. How dare you make these accusations?"

I shook my head. "It was you who locked us in the shed. You knew we'd been talking with Brody. And your nephew probably told you about getting attacked by a girl and a guy with flashlights, and getting whacked by another girl with a cast." I held out my arm.

Nico fired a blazing stare in my direction.

"You probably saw us going into the fields, and when we slipped into the building you locked us in. My brother saw you walking away from the shed."

His eyes raged like flames and his nostrils flared. "You will all be sorry you've made such ridiculous claims." Nico glared at me. "You are a nosey little girl, and you will pay for prying."

Brody stepped forward. "No one's going to pay except you, Nico. You can air your complaints to the police." He waved his phone. "I'm sure they'll be very interested in your explanation of what's been going on. They'll be here any moment."

Serena covered her mouth.

Brody moved to her side and placed his hands on her shoulders. "I'm so sorry."

She looked up at him. "I'm glad you and the kids figured this out." She sighed. "My father is going to be horribly disappointed in Nico." She bulleted a piercing stare at him. Then she gazed at Brody, a slight smile caressing her lips. "But he'll be very proud of you, Brody."

After returning the smile, he focused on me. Brody reached out, touched my arm and winked. "Good job, Leilani."

Kanakolukumamakolu
(Thirty-Three)

I'd done it!

"Way cool, Leilani." Sam poked my shoulder.

Maile grabbed my arm with one hand and shoved the other high in the air. "The Hawaiian Island Detective Club lives on!"

The police had arrived and were talking with Nico, Brody, Serena and Drew.

Maile danced around us. "Did you see Nico's face when you nailed him? Majorly scared me. I thought his eyes were going to turn into lasers and he'd zap us dead right there. And if that didn't kill us, the fire coming from his mouth would have. I shook so hard, my legs nearly collapsed."

"True story." Sam nodded. "Maile grabbed me and almost took me to the ground with her."

Nico's expression seemed etched in my mind — maybe imprinted there forever. "Yeah, I pretty much ignored all the fireworks going on inside my body. Otherwise, I would have fainted, or thrown up on Nico's shoes."

Maile giggled. "I kinda like that picture. Horrified and speechless, just staring at the mess on his feet." She imitated a not-so-happy Nico.

Sam bellowed and I shook my head, glad we could find the

whole experience entertaining.

Brody approached. "You kids did a great job. I'll talk with the police now, but I'm sure they'll contact you later. Do you have a ride home?"

"I need to call my mom." Sam peered down the hall. "Do you think the receptionist will let us use the phone?"

"Here." Brody extended his cell. "Use mine."

After Sam talked with his mom, we galloped down the hall, burst through the door and trucked outside, still bubbling with excitement.

Energized, yet exhausted, we dumped ourselves into chairs on the huge lanai. I settled my head into the cushion and breathed in the sweet pineapple scent wafting from the fields.

Maile passed us a sideways glance. "Did you hear what Serena said?"

Sam smirked. "Oh, yeah! The reward. She promised it would be coming. We were great detectives — especially you, Leilani. You were smart and totally brave, especially with the whole stakeout thing...for a girl, anyway." He snatched a breath. "Hey, Leilani, tell Kimo how important he was in solving the mystery."

Maile and I laughed.

"What?"

I shrugged. "Nothing. You're just super cool, that's all."

He gave us a little lip-curl. "Whatever."

"So what are you two going to buy with your reward money?" Maile frowned. "My mom will probably tell me to put it in my savings for college."

"Yeah, mine too." I pressed my lips tight. "But hopefully I can convince her to let me use part of it to buy a second surfboard. I still want a soft-top."

"Hey! There's my mom. She'll freak when we tell her what happened." Sam jogged to the car.

We piled inside and babbled during the entire ride to my house. Explaining to Mrs. Bennett what happened was difficult. Mostly, we confused her. Didn't matter. We knew what had happened, and I was proud of the three of us.

Even after we'd arrived at my house, my heart continued thumping like a crazed drummer in my chest. Had I ever been this excited about anything before? "Thanks for the ride, Mrs. Bennett." I slipped out of the car.

"No problem." Sam's mom leaned her head out the window. "Oh, and congratulations on figuring out whatever it was you figured out at the plantation."

Grinning, I waved goodbye to Maile and Sam.

Although energized on the inside, on the outside I was barely able to drag myself into the house. Hungry and exhausted, I lost the physical battle and just wanted to collapse onto my bed. A mango sitting in the fruit basket caught my attention. I grabbed it, pulled away some skin and sank my teeth into the delicious treat. Juice dribbled down my chin as I lumbered to my room. I entered, then stopped and stared.

My cell phone sat in the middle of the bed, a note resting next to it.

Sorry, sweetie!

Here's your cell. I'd rather you have a phone, and risk you forgetting it once in a while. I figure that's much better than you never having back-up in case of emergency.

I love you, Mom

She'd drawn a little heart at the end.

My mouth curved. I loved Mom too.

I set the note and phone on my nightstand, snuggled into my pillow and finished devouring the sweet fruit. My mind swirled with images from the day. I could hardly wait for Mom and Kimo to come home. How would I explain everything to them? I'd probably be so excited, I'd just blurt it out in a b'zillion muddled words.

I had to admit, when Kimo wasn't annoying or goofy, he was pretty amazing. Not only did he help us with clues, he saved us from our prison in the pineapple fields. Guess, once in a while, he could be a special blessing from God. I burrowed deeper into my cozy covers and grinned. But, most of the time, Kimo was still my pain-in-the-pants little brother.

I must have fallen asleep because, the next thing I knew, I awoke to honking. Curious, I ventured outside to see who was making the obnoxious noise.

Kainoa.

One last blast of the horn, then he waved to me. What was he doing here? I thought he'd never talk to me again. I took a step toward the truck.

He jumped out and headed to the back. "Hey, Leilani, I have something for you." He reached into the bed and pulled out my surfboard. A smile overtook my lips. Even though I still couldn't use it, I loved having my treasure back home. He placed it against the house.

I reached to caress the smooth surfboard deck, but Kainoa stepped between me and my red and white beauty. "Leilani, I need to explain something. It's about Carly."

My insides churned like hot magma when I pictured Carly Rivers. My heart ached knowing Kainoa wouldn't believe me about her part in the vandalism.

"The other day, when I was going to meet Carly for a lesson, I spotted her from a distance. She was screaming about you and taking revenge against your board…and…" He stepped aside.

"There's a huge ding!"

"She thrashed like a crazy, obsessed person." A groan escaped Kainoa's mouth. "She pounded her fists against your board, kicked at it, and threw some rocks and a coconut before I could catch up to her. I'm so sorry."

Gulping, I touched my fingers to the damage.

"But I can repair it." He sighed. "Would have fixed it before bringing the board back, but figured you wouldn't trust me." He lowered his chin and stared at the ground. "When I saw Carly purposely damaging your surfboard, I knew you were right. She was involved in the pineapple vandalism." He leveled his eyes with mine. "I'm sorry I didn't believe you. You've always been a super great friend to Maile. I should have known you –"

I held up my hand. "Stop, Kainoa. It's okay, I understand. And I totally trust you to repair the ding."

"Cool." A crooked smile crossed his lips and he sighed as if relieved. "See? You're totally amazing."

I couldn't think of a thing to say.

"Maile told me all about you solving the mystery of the pineapple fields."

I just gawked at him with what was probably a silly grin. Suddenly, my cheeks burned. Were they red? Did he notice?

"Whoa, 'mos forgit. Stay hea an' I git dakine."

"'kay." I stayed put, but wondered what he'd forgotten.

Kainoa plodded to his truck and opened the passenger door. He reached in, pulled something from the seat, then turned and jogged toward me.

I gasped. He was holding a beautiful pink plumeria lei.

Kainoa draped it over my head and situated the lei on my shoulders so it dropped down in the back as well as the front. "Mahalo, Leilani."

Then he kissed my cheek.

Book Two
Menehunes Missing
Coming Soon!

It's just a game, right?

Wrong! *The Menehune Hunt* turns into eerie intrigue filled with danger as The Hawaiian Island Detective Club tackles their second genuine mystery.

The crazy clues make no sense at all, but Leilani is determined to figure out why the statues of Hawaii's treasured, Leprechaun-like little people are disappearing during the school fundraiser event, even if it means asking her pain-in-the-pants, ten-year-old brother, Kimo, for help.

A fire, a visit from police, a creepy stakeout, too many suspects and an intense diversion involving Kimo and an irate storeowner hinders their investigation. Leilani worries that they'll never figure out who's stealing the odd, yet unremarkable little statues, and why.

Are she and her friends in danger ... possibly from someone they know?

From Chapter One of
Menehunes Missing

I smoothed the crumpled paper, stared at the words and read the first clue.

I'm Menehune Number One. Find and check me out if you can.
I'm hiding amongst kids and cords.

Maile Onakea and Sam Bennett, my best friends, burst into my room.

Sam jumped onto my bed, his shaggy blonde hair flopping around like palm fronds in the wind. "Did you get it? I'm crazy pumped about this whole Menehune Hunt thing. Bet no matter how hard the clue is, you've already figured it out, huh? Come on, Leilani! Read that puppy out loud."

Maile giggled. "Sam, you're insane." She plopped onto my bed, tucked a strand of her long hair behind her ear, and locked dark brown eyes on mine. "So, what does it say?"

I ignored her question. "You guys sure got here fast."

"My mom and I picked up Sam, then came straight to your house. Mom thinks it's cool we're doing the statue search thing."

I nodded. "So does mine. She says the money raised will

really help the school. Guess there've been a couple hundred people who've already paid the entry fee." I pictured myself starting eighth grade with a computer room full of brand new equipment.

Sam groaned. "Okay, so everyone's mom is happy. No need to party about it. Show us the clue. Let's get on this wave and ride it all the way. We have a totally great chance of winning because we're amazing at solving stuff. Just like the whole pineapple mystery. So, get on it, Leilani — We're waiting."

CPSIA information can be obtained at www.ICGtesting.com
Printed in the USA
BVOW080113130712

295068BV00005B/5/P

9 781938 388156